Mary Botham Howitt

Alice Franklin - a Tale

Mary Botham Howitt

Alice Franklin - a Tale

ISBN/EAN: 9783337088545

Printed in Europe, USA, Canada, Australia, Japan

Cover: Foto ©Andreas Hilbeck / pixelio.de

More available books at **www.hansebooks.com**

ALICE FRANKLIN.

A Tale.

———•———

ANOTHER PART OF

"SOWING AND REAPING."

———•———

BY MARY HOWITT.

AUTHOR OF "STRIVE AND THRIVE;" "HOPE ON, HOPE EVER;"
"NO SENSE LIKE COMMON SENSE," &C., &C.

NEW-YORK:

D. APPLETON & COMPANY,

443 & 445 BROADWAY.

M.DCCC.LXIII.

CONTENTS.

ALICE FRANKLIN.

CHAPTER I.

FRIENDS BY THE FIRESIDE.

THERE were many great dinner-parties and costly entertainments in London on the evening of a certain 18th of October; not that it was any day of public and general festivity, but there is not a day throughout the year in which, in London, this is not the case; and, besides the grand and the expensive, there were others too of a very different character, in which the five or the ten shillings, which were to provide the little entertainment for the two or three dear friends, had been spared with difficulty out of the month's or week's allowance. To our minds nothing can be more affecting than these little sacrifices to friendship and affection. Would to God that anxiety and care did not too often come in also as guests with the invited!

Let us then see, on this afternoon of the 18th of October, Elizabeth Durant enter the humble lodgings of herself and her mother, with the small basket of purchases which was to serve for the entertainment of three friends.

B

" I would not invite people at all," said her mother, who was sitting in her large chair by the fire, " if I could not entertain them handsomely."

" Nor would I," replied Elizabeth; " nor do I, except Alice and her mother, and Mr. Netley; they know us so well that I never pretend to get any thing out of the way for them. They would fare quite as well, if not better, at home; but then there is a sentiment of good fellowship which they would feel if they only took bread and water with us. I make some little sacrifice to entertain them thus simply; this they know, and for this reason they always seem happy when they come."

" *Seem so*," repeated her mother. " Yes, they seem so out of charity; I hate people to be civil to one out of charity!"

Elizabeth smiled, and went on with her little arrangements, for she was used to her mother's infirmity of temper, and she had great forbearance with her.

Poor Mrs. Durant, however, was sadly out of sorts to-day, and she did not long maintain silence. " I wonder how you can be contented to live as we do," said she, " you a gentlewoman born and bred—but you never had my spirit! You have done very wrong, Elizabeth—very foolishly! You may wait long enough before you get such another offer!"

Elizabeth knew well enough to what her mother alluded; it was a painful cause of difference between them, and had been so for the last three months.

" Dearest mother," returned Elizabeth, " have you yet to learn that most common-place of all truisms, that money alone cannot make married life happy?"

"It cannot be happy without it," retorted her mother.

"I never will so far sell myself as to marry merely for a home, whilst I have the ability to maintain myself," replied Elizabeth.

"By maintaining yourself," returned her mother "you are cut off from any good connexion;—such foolish or otherwise, are the prejudices of society. A man of rank would no sooner think of marrying the maker of artificial flowers than his cook—you have no chance of that kind. Besides this, you ought to take into consideration that you are not as young now as you have been; every additional year tells upon you now, to which you must add the effect and influence of narrow circumstances, and the anxiety which they necessarily bring—for you cannot, you see, even ask your friends to drink a miserable cup of tea without stinting yourself for it one way or another; and then, if you become ill or infirm, what is to become of you?"

Elizabeth sighed.

"Yes, as I was saying," continued her mother, "every year will add wrinkles and gray hairs; and then where will be the man with fifty thousand pounds, who will beg and pray, and beg and pray again, for you to be his wife? I tell you what, Elizabeth, you have been a great fool."

"How often," said Elizabeth, pausing in the midst of her little preparations, "must I assure you that I could not have been even tolerably happy with Mr. Watson? Take your own view of the case—you who reason so much from the argument of being a gentlewoman born and bred. Here is a man, coarse and vulgar in appearance and manners, of no education—a common baker, who brings bread to our own door. Was he a fit husband for me, though in a worldly point of view I was not higher than he? We both had to get our daily bread, whilst I was subjected to many more self-denials and much more bitter experience of a low estate than he, because his mind, his tastes, his habits, were all suited to his own class. You thought, as I did, that he was very unfit for my husband—that his very proposal had something of presumption in it. A fortnight afterwards, the merest chance in the world, the drawing of a fortunate lottery number, makes him the possessor of fifty thousand pounds. He is then rich, is then unquestionably, in a worldly point of view, my superior, and though I could not but acknowledge some degree of generosity and sincerity in his again renewing his suit, the man, in mind and manners, remained the same—I could not marry him."

"The greater fool you!" returned her mother. "Fifty thousand pounds! You have no idea of the value of money; then as to the man himself—the very possession of wealth refines any one!"

"You yourself," replied Elizabeth, "look down on upstart tradespeople—on parvenu gentry."

"All London is made up of parvenu gentry!" said her mother. "You'll die poor," continued she—"die perhaps in a workhouse;—for what is to become of you when you get old and infirm, or blind, or when flowers go out of fashion—which they may any day?"

Again Elizabeth sighed, for she did not need to be reminded of these things; but as she had always carefully avoided talking on painful anxieties to her mother, her mother never knew what she really felt.

" And then," continued her mother, " if you are so disinterested as not to think much for yourself, you might think a little for other people—for me, for instance. What's to become of me if anything should happen to Lady Thicknisse ?—or she may take it into her head to stop my annuity ; she is old, and wilful, and fanciful—she has quarrelled, you know, even with Sir Lynam."

" Your annuity is safe as long as she lives," said Elizabeth ; " and after that," continued she, with a tearful eye, " I have firm faith in the goodness of God that we shall not want."

" Many good people do want, though," said her mother ; " and this I know, that God helps those who help themselves. You have flung away such a chance as you will not again have; he'll not come begging and praying to you again."

" Most likely not," said Elizabeth.

" Positively not !" returned her mother, provoked by her apparent imperturbability ; " and I'll tell you what, Elizabeth, it was only yesterday that I was silly enough to go all the way to Hammersmith to see his fine house there. I had heard about it—you look surprised—I had heard about it, I say, and about something else besides, and I had a mind to see him if I could."

" Surely, surely not," exclaimed Elizabeth, fearful what her mother's motives might have been.

" Don't alarm yourself," said her mother ; " I did not see him, at least, not to speak to him, but I saw his house—as proper a gentleman's house as I would wish to see—not an old, stately place, like Stanton Combe, but a handsome substantial place, I can assure you, and fit for a Durant to have married into. I was fool enough to give a shilling to the house-keeper to show me over it: it had all been furnished new—she said the furniture alone cost many thousands—"

" Why did you do so?" asked Elizabeth, mortified and distressed. " I would not for the world that he should know what you have done!"

" Bless my life, child!" returned her mother; " he is not likely to know—he's married."

" I was right, then," said Elizabeth, smiling. " I told you he would soon get over his disappointment."

" Married he is," continued her mother, " and to a gentlewoman, too—to a banker's daughter out of Leicestershire, I think they said—with twenty thousand pounds expectations. They happened to arrive just before I went away—in a carriage-and-four— and a very pretty young girl she was! God forgive me," said poor Mrs. Durant, with a sigh, " I could not help breaking one of the commandments—for I coveted her lot for you."

" I would rather," said Elizabeth, " even after all you have told me, gain my daily bread by my own fingers, and keep my firm reliance on Providence, than have married Mr. Watson with all his wealth. Marriage is the most holy of God's ordinances, and we sin against him when we marry without love. I did not refuse him, I assure you, without having deeply weighed the matter, and I felt that I dared not to have married him—feeling towards him, and thinking of him, as I did."

" As I have told you scores of times," argued her mother, " you don't understand these things ; children would have **been a bond of** love between you ; love would have slid into your heart you know not how!"

Elizabeth shook her head as if in doubt—but smiled nevertheless. She made no reply, but went **on with her little arrangements, and** then, when all was ready, sat down to her **work till the arrival of** her guests. In the mean time her mother had been **still** thinking on topics **akin to the old subject, and** no sooner was her daughter **seated than she resumed the conversation.** " And I must say," said she, as if merely continuing the train of her own thoughts, " that Philip **has** behaved very shamefully **to you,** and yet, some way or other, you never seem to feel it as you ought to do." This, too, was **a subject of** difference between **Elizabeth and her mother,** and was even more painful to her **than the former.** " But there really is something so strange **about you," con-**tinued she ; " **a woman of spirit would have thought** so differently."

" What right had **I," asked Elizabeth, " to resent Philip's conduct, or even** to think it **faulty ? Heaven knows how** much we have to thank him for ; and **you know as well as I do how much he has suffered on our account."**

" **And he** knows," argued Mrs. Durant, " how much we have all suffered from his father ;—we have been made homeless, penniless—we have been reduced to beggary, through the tyranny of his father ; and he, who always professed to see things so differently to him, ought to have made us **some amends if it had been in his power."**

" Amends ! " repeated Elizabeth. " But, my dear mother, you overlook so many things—you take a partial view of so many things—and you forget so much of the past. I was but a mere child when all the first troubles began at Stanton Combe, but I think Sir Thomas Durant had no hand in them. That he profited by our misfortunes I grant—but if he had not, some one else, it is probable, would ; and even in that case he was counteracted by Richard ; Richard left the place a heap of ruins to his hand."

" And he did right ! " exclaimed Mrs. Durant, warmly.

" We think so differently on so many subjects," said Elizabeth, sorrowfully—" why do we continually talk of them ? If we studiously endeavoured to create a difference between us, we could not do otherwise."

" I want to create no difference between us," returned her mother ; "but I must say that I am aggravated when I think of these things, and see how little spirit you show ! Then as to what Philip Durant has done for us," continued she, pertinaciously clinging to these painful thoughts, " he has taken Richard from me—made an exile of him for life ; and whether he lives or dies is more than I can tell."

" Cannot you see," replied Elizabeth, " what a blessing it is that he is provided for, and that he is far better out of England than in it ? He made himself, unfortunately, amenable to the law ; and the very man who has suffered through him has provided for him ; and it has now been his own fault if he have not, in some measure, retrieved his own life, at least as far as himself was concerned."

" So long as I thought Philip intended to take the place of son to me," replied Mrs. Durant, " and to provide for you, by marrying you, as was no more than his duty, I was satisfied ; but I soon saw that he had no such intention ; and with all his coming here, and his professions, he never had—and that provokes me ! "

" I wish," said Elizabeth, " that you never had taken up the idea of Philip marrying me. I have told you all along, that neither he nor I had a thought of the kind. He has been my best, my kindest friend—more to me than a brother—and such, I hope, he will always remain ; but he was too honourable a man to marry me when he was engaged to another."

" And what was that other?" returned Mrs. Durant. " A girl without a penny—a teacher in a school."

" A high-minded, high-principled woman—a gentleman's daughter—and one worthy of him in every respect!" interposed Elizabeth, with warmth. "Philip would have been a dishonourable man to have deserted her from any chivalric notions of honour towards us. He has, as it is, done more for us than we had any right to expect—besides which, you seem to forget that he has ruined himself, at least for the present, with his father, because he screened Richard from his vengeance."

" The old tyrant ! " said Mrs. Durant, between her teeth.

" For two years," continued Elizabeth, " he has never seen his father, who sternly rejects all attempts at reconciliation ; and considering Philip's remarkable attachment to his father, without looking at it in a worldly point of view, this is no small punishment.

Poor Philip!" said she, with a deep sigh: " his prospects in life are not by any means bright at present;
think only of his wife and child!"

" Well," returned Mrs. Durant, " what a fool he
was to marry—to marry a penniless woman without
his father's consent.   He might, at all events, have
waited till he had made his peace with him."

" Philip's marriage, as you know," said Elizabeth,
" was hurried on by Gertrude's unhappy situation.
She was ill,—God knows, but I fear she will not live
many years.   It was not wise, perhaps—but then,
consider : she was in an unprosperous school, where
she had too much to do, and where she was even
stinted in food ; her health gave way; the physicians
ordered her, as she valued her life, to return to her
friends ; she had no friend but the widow of her
uncle, who had been her guardian, and who had
married a second husband with grown-up sons and
daughters. The particulars of all this I know only in
part; but this I know, that Philip, like a kind-hearted,
generous, uncalculating, and unworldly man as he is,
married her—although, in his peculiar circumstances,
at variance with his father as he then was, it was
anything but prudent.   They married ; and their
fortunes, as is natural, are not flattering ; still in
each other they are blessed as human beings can
be.   You yourself know that ; you yourself, dearest
mother," said Elizabeth, with a beautiful smile, " like
Gertrude, and acknowledge her to be a most lovely
creature."

" It has been a most foolish piece of business altogether," said Mrs. Durant, who was in too ill a
humour to concede anything ; "and I hate secrets and

mysteries of any **kind.** Philip had no business **to** have married, and that I shall still continue to say. I am not pleased with him—and not even an arch- angel himself will ever persuade me out of **my own** common **sense.**"

Mrs. Durant said what was true—nothing in **this** world would ever have reconciled her to the idea of Philip having done right in marrying other than Elizabeth. It had been the favourite idea of the unhappy lady's head for many months after her first acquaintance with him. She had begun to take more cheerful views of life in consequence of it. She had sat, times innumerable, and built up castles in the **air** based on this foundation. Her very heart had warmed to her daughter, less for her many meek virtues, her indefatigable kindness, and her self-denying affection, than as the imagined wife of the future **Sir Philip** Durant, as the mistress of a future Stanton **Combe,** which, like a phœnix, was to rise out of the ashes of the former, and to afford under its broad ample **roof** a shelter not only for herself but **for her** exiled Richard, who, according to her wishes, was **to return** like the infant Jesus out of Egypt, **when they were** **dead who had** sought his life, and **who** was to occa- sion **and** to deserve far more rejoicing than even the prodigal son of the Gospel.

Poor Mrs. Durant! she had never told Elizabeth one-hundredth part of her speculations; and thus, when the bridegroom elect of her own heart married another, she felt like one injured, **and** as if **she** really had been duped in some way or other. She never, therefore, **spoke or** thought of this subject without being angry.

In the midst of these undesirable feelings, the glass-coach drove up to the door, containing the three expected guests. But guests of so much importance must be introduced with a new chapter.

CHAPTER II.

GOLDEN PROMISES.

IT is now some years since we saw Mrs. Franklin and her daughter Alice—scarcely indeed have we seen them since that time when, refusing her daughter as wife for the lawyer Sharple, she was obliged to leave the house of Sir Thomas Durant. Let us consider. It is about six years since that time; Alice was then eighteen, and consequently now four-and-twenty. A year or so the junior of Elizabeth Durant, in appearance several years so—Alice, in fact, did not look above twenty—things had gone on smoothly with her:—she knew, from her own experience, real care no more than did the Sybarite who complained of the crushed rose-leaf.

Alice Franklin and Elizabeth Durant were dear friends, and had been so ever since they became acquainted, although of characters most opposite. Had Elizabeth resembled Alice, they must have clashed and severed long ago; had Alice resembled Elizabeth, they must have been fast friends for life; as it was, they had not been sufficiently tried, and therefore they remained friends.

At eighteen, Alice had been called by her stern

uncle "well-grown and passingly handsome." The
opinion of the world was, that she was beautiful.
Beautiful she certainly was—of a patrician style of
beauty ; of a tall, bending gracefulness, which resembled a white lily. Her features were exquisitely
chiselled ; her head gracefully set on beautiful
shoulders ; her eyes, though not remarkably large,
were finely formed, and of that clear dark gray colour
which at times, from their extraordinary brightness,
leaves the beholder uncertain of their exact hue ; her
hair was of the softest chestnut brown, and was worn
in long, unconfined ringlets, in a style which, while
it suited her face and figure, is perhaps, generally
speaking, more picturesque than becoming.

In character she was a singular mixture of sentiment and coldness—was romantic and calculating at
the same time. She herself esteemed Elizabeth
rather than loved her—she would have loved her
more if she had not been morally so superior to herself. Elizabeth loved her rather than esteemed her ;
she was aware of her faults, but she loved her as a
sister spite of those faults. Alice felt that if ever she
fell into adversity, Elizabeth would stand by her, true
to death. Elizabeth doubted whether, if fortune and
the world showered their smiles and favours on Alice,
she would not soon forsake, if not disown her. Still,
however, all as yet had been an untroubled calm,
and their friendship had been like a happy sunshiny day. Alice had no other female friend than
Elizabeth, and she opened her heart to her as much
as it was possible for her to open it to any one ; she,
in reality, professed more affection for her than in
her own soul she knew she felt, and Elizabeth be-

lieved her, because in every word and deed she her self was so sincere.

Alice Franklin, whilst she appeared perfectly natural, was one of the most artificial of human beings; nobody knew but herself how every attitude, every action had been studied, and was suited to time and place. People saw her sitting, and it seemed to them that they saw an exquisite picture; "she could not have sat better for her portrait, and that rich crimson curtain behind her produces so fine an effect!" Ah, artful Alice Franklin, but for that crimson cur tain, and that low seat, she would not have sat there. She knew how to rise, how to stand, how to move for effect, yet no one would ever have suspected her of all this; for her art was the most consummate of all— it never betrayed itself. She was, besides this, pos sessed of much natural talent; drew, danced, sang, played—if not like a master, at least with so much effect that it was all the same. Money, leisure, and some degree of ambition, had done for her all that could be done. Her mother doted on her beyond words; she was, in her eyes, perfection itself. Her grand-uncle Netley, too, whilst he cherished for her the warmest affection, and whose heiress, of course, she was always considered, not only by others, but by himself, saw, however, deeper into the real springs of her character than any one else; and for this reason, in the bottom of her soul, she did not quite like him. His silent penetration wounded both her self-love and her pride. No third person, however, would in the slightest degree have suspected her of the least want of affection towards him, nor outwardly did she ever fail the least in duty and respect. She was too much alive to the world's opinion for that. The world knew, as well as she did, not only what were her and her mother's obligations to this kind relative, but what were their expectations from him ; outwardly, therefore, all was smooth and pleasant, and amiable as an angel's self. Yes, artful indeed was the fair Alice Franklin !

One other trait of character we must give, and then we will leave her to act and speak for herself. She was, as we have said, romantic ; had romantic notions and views of life, which seemed almost at variance with her really cold and prudential heart. She was superstitious too ; had great faith in dreams, presages and omens ; and was one of those persons to whom singular passages and accidents occurred, as if to stagger one's sober judgment and perplex one's unbelief.

Such a girl as Alice Franklin had, of course, many lovers, the accepted among whom was Henry Maitland, the son of a prosperous gold-and-silversmith of the city. Henry Maitland was deeply and desperately in love, and had been so for two whole years. His family, who were all charmed with Alice, wished the marriage to take place : so did both her mother and Mr. Netley ; but Alice delayed and delayed ; she would assign no reason why, but that she would not yet—the next winter, or the next summer, whatever the season might then be, but not yet ! And Alice had her way, while good Mr. Netley thought within himself that Alice loved not truly, or she would not thus tantalise her promised bridegroom ; and, in his own mind, he said that he should not at all wonder if the marriage never took place. He

did not know why, but someway or other he thought
it would not—and such an idea always made him
angry with her.

No sooner had Alice taken off her glove, than
Elizabeth missed a certain beautiful ring from her
hand, which had been given to her by her lover
under peculiar circumstances, and which Elizabeth
knew she made a point of always wearing. Alice
said nothing of the ring, but began to tell how she
had had her fortune told that morning by a deaf and
dumb sybil, and that, according to her report, she
was on the eve of a great change in fortune; a letter
was on the way to her, and she was to darken somebody's path in life; she was to have a deal of trouble
herself, and yet to be very fortunate. She said that
someway or other it had made her very low-spirited.

"Besides which," said Mr. Netley, who had been
listening to her words, "she has broken Henry's ring
to-day."

Alice held up her beautiful hand to show the absence of the ring, which her friend had noticed
already.

"It is the second time," said Alice, "that it has
broken. It broke as Henry put it on my finger first;
it broke again this morning, without any apparent
cause, as I was playing with it. One piece seemed to
fall to the ground, but though I have spent hours in
the search, I have not been able to find it." It por-
tended some dire misfortune, she was persuaded.

All laughed at the superstitious girl, and declared
that she had already experienced the misfortune which
it foretold, in the loss of the ring itself.

After tea, Mrs. Durant began to tell how she had

gone the day before to see the ex-baker's house at Hammersmith, and astonished them by the news of his marriage with the banker's fair daughter, who, she said, with a look of bitter reproach at Elizabeth, " was wiser than some people, and who had not thought herself too good for his wife."

" Only think," continued the poor lady, who could not rid herself of the haunting idea, " how different it would have been if we, on this very evening, had been sitting in that handsomely-furnished house—you the mistress of some thousands a year, with servants to wait on you, and with no care or anxiety at all! I'll be bound to say he would have let you launch out into what expense you liked, for he would have looked up to you in all knowledge of life; and you might have had all your old friends about you, as much as you had wished, for he would have been so glad to have got into better society. What a difference there would then have been! Ah, child!" said she, in a tone of unspeakable vexation, " you have been the greatest fool under the sun!"

There was some little difference of opinion on this subject. Mr. Netley thought that low people, suddenly raised to wealth, were often the most unmanageable, impracticable people; he did not think, as he had said before, that had Elizabeth married the ex-baker, he would at all have given up the reins to his wife. From what he knew of the man, he said, he never expected him to run through his money foolishly. as many did—he expected whoever lived twenty years, and knew him then, would find him a miserly curmudgeon, who, ignorant himself, and naturally narrow-minded, would begrudge his children education, and thus, to use a common proverb, lay up rods in pickle for himself in his old age.

Alice and her mother were **warmly** unanimous in saying that the fifty thousand pounds, could it have been taken without the ex-baker, would have been **most desirable; but as** it was, they would have done **like Elizabeth—would have** preferred making artificial flowers to have been Mrs. Watson.

From this subject **the** conversation turned **on** the **influence** which sudden and great wealth has on the heart and character. Alice, like the ex-baker, had often tried her luck in lotteries, and all agreed that, **if faith** was to be put **in** the deaf and dumb sybil, she **too was to be** fortunate **in** the numbers she had to **draw.** Her uncle said that sudden wealth was mostly a misfortune, **and** he gave many instances to support **his opinion.**

" **Yes,**" said Elizabeth, " I grant all you say to be **true in those** particular instances; but you have **looked merely** on weak minds, cold, selfish hearts, **who were** incapable of acting otherwise; but can you **not imagine** instances in which sudden and even enormous **wealth might be** possessed with humility, and used worthily? Is there no human heart, I do not **say able to** resist all temptation, but in which natural **goodness is** not strong enough to keep it at least **tolerably right,** even under great temptation?"

Mr. Netley demurred. " Suppose any one of us **now,"** said he, " were to be the drawer of one of your **great prizes?**"

" Oh," said Alice, with **a** glow which, if it were not generous emotion, most strongly resembled it, **"if** such were my fortune, how happy would not I

make you all! Elizabeth, you should share it with
me—we would live like second ladies of Llangollen in
a beautiful cottage together—you should then never
spend your life in making artificial flowers!"

"But Mr. Maitland?" said Elizabeth, smiling.
"One of the ladies in the cottage would have to leave
for a husband."

"Well, I only wish," returned Alice, "that I
might be tried."

"If gold does not rust," said Mr. Netley gravely,
"there is an innate principle of corruption in it—it
corrupts its possessor."

"I would gladly take the wealth," returned Alice,
"without fear of its consequences on myself—I
should like to be tried."

"Elizabeth has resisted it—has rejected it," said
the old gentleman.

"Yes," replied Alice, "I can very well understand
why she rejected it in that case; if she could have
taken the money without the man, it would have been
very different. However, if my numbers are lucky,
I'll take care of Elizabeth, "said she, taking her hand
affectionately, "for she deserves it; and all that
Mrs. Durant says is very true—it is, it must be, a
hopeless thing to work for one's own bread."

"I am sure, if Alice had the means, she would do
all she says," remarked her mother.

"My life, however, is not as hopeless as you
think," said Elizabeth; "for though I, for myself, have
no expectation of fortune either from one quarter or
another, still I possess that which is better than such
expectation, and that is confidence in the goodness of
Providence: He will not let either myself or my mother

want. I look for no other than a life of labour for my
self—God grant me only patience and ability for it!"

"And that you will have!" said good Mr. Netley,
with warmth.

"I wish more than that," said Alice; "I wish to
Heaven I might be your benefactor." Tears were in
her eyes as she said this, and the generosity of the
sentiment gave an almost angelic expression to her
countenance.

Never had these two families seemed more united
than they were this evening. Poor Mrs. Durant herself forgot some of her vexations, when she saw so
many kind faces beaming around her in the bright
fire-light. She could not help feeling glad that there
were some in the great city who would now and then
come in and drink a friendly and unexpensive cup of
tea with them.

At eight o'clock Alice's lover, who knew of their
being here, joined them; and though she told him of
the broken ring, and repeated her belief in its evil
portent, never had she seemed kinder to him—never
happier, and never gayer, than she was that evening.

"What a bewitching creature she is!" said Mrs.
Durant to her daughter, when the glass-coach which
had brought them carried them home again at ten
o'clock. "If you had only been as handsome as she
is, what a lucky thing it would have been! Her
face would be her fortune without any other. I pro-
test she gets handsomer every day, and how fond poor
Maitland is of her!"

"_Poor!_" repeated Elizabeth.

"Ay, _poor_," returned her mother; "someway or
other I always feel sorry for him—he seems such an

excellent young man, and so dotingly fond of her—
and she has a world of pride, that she has—she often
treats him like a dog."

Elizabeth smiled, and said that one day Mr. Netley
had called him Jemmy Grove, and she ' the scornful
Barbara Allen.'

" Ah, well !" said Mrs. Durant ; " but, bless me !
what a fine prospect she has—I would not wish anything better for you, than to be a rich tradesman's
wife ! "

" Leave off wishing for me," said Elizabeth ; " you
only by doing so create disappointment and dissatisfaction for yourself. Try to be satisfied with me as
I am ; and let us both endeavour to be contented
with our own destiny, for that is the true philosophy
of life."

" I never was much of a philosopher," said poor
Mrs. Durant ; " and it's now too late in the day for
me to attempt it."

CHAPTER III.

LETTERS AND NEWS.

WE must now, with our reader's permission, look
backward a few years, and pay a visit to the old Hall
of Starkey, in the palatinate of Durham.

After Mrs. Durant fell into misfortune, the friendship between herself and Lady Thicknisse began to
decline, which perhaps was only natural, more especially as Lady Thicknisse never concealed the dis-

satisfaction which she felt in the conduct of her god-son, Richard. The annuity which she allowed to Mrs. Durant was paid quarterly with undeviating punctuality; but the acknowledgment of this, which at first was made equally regularly, was before long discontinued, in consequence of a remark of Lady Thicknisse herself, which she wrote, too, with her own hand, as a postscript to one of her sister-in-law, Mrs. Betty's, letters, to this purpose,—" that seeing Mrs. Durant could not command franks, these acknowledgments were a needless cost of postage, particularly as Mrs. Durant herself would take care that the London banker was not remiss in his payment."

There had been a time when Mrs. Durant would have resented such a slight on her correspondence, even from Lady Thicknisse; but that time was long gone by. Mrs. Durant was not what she had been; so, though she was offended and hurt, she let the affront sleep, with the mortifying remark to herself, " that beggars cannot be choosers," and in future received her quarterly payment without so much as thanking either banker or banker's clerk.

Intercourse, however, with Starkey was not at an end; for good Mrs. Betty, who never in all her life before had been a letter-writer, took up her pen as her stately sister-in-law laid down hers, and availed herself of a frank now and then, or of a private opportunity, to prove to her well-beloved god-daughter that she was not forgotten.

Poor Mrs. Durant laughed contemptuously, when Mrs. Betty's first letter arrived: " For," said she, " what can she find to write about, when she knows nothing of Lady Thicknisse's movements, and how in the world will she write, who never in the whole course of her life wrote half-a-dozen letters!"

But dear Mrs. Betty wrote as she talked, and while Elizabeth read them, it seemed as if the very tone of her voice accompanied the words. Some people have the gift of writing thus naturally, and a great gift it is; and if one loves the writer, how doubly valuable are such letters! Mrs. Betty Thicknisse, unlettered and simple-minded as she was, wrote in this style, and her letters, therefore, always were interesting to Elizabeth, and in process of time, when they began to tell of the goings-on at Starkey, became interesting to her mother also.

Our readers may probably remember what was stated in our former volume, viz., that after the sudden death of the late Sir Sampson, who left no descendants, the title, together with the Hertfordshire estate, passed to the heir-at-law, Lynam Thicknisse, then a child—the rich property of Starkey itself still remaining in the possession of the widow of Sir Sampson, from reasons which for many years remained a mystery to the public.

Sir Lynam, as a boy, had passed all his school holidays at Starkey, and in the intervals of his college life he and his tutor were there also. But by degrees the visits, which at first had only been a cause of pleasure and pride to the mistress of the mansion, became less agreeable. Sir Lynam was wild and wilful, and, as he grew old, became more unmanageable in temper, and more unrestrained in action, till at length the poor lady came to the conclusion, drawn from experience both of her adopted son, Lynam, and

her godson, Richard Durant, that the present generation of young men was wofully degenerated. Much,
too, as she had always protested and believed that
she loved Sir Lynam, she found that as he grew
older, and worse, she in reality cared very little about
him. She dismissed him, therefore, from Starkey,
during one college vacation, assuring him that she
would not henceforth have her repose disturbed by
his riot, and that, therefore, if he chose, after he had
sown his wild college oats, still to shoot over the
manors of Starkey, he must locate himself somewhere
quietly in the neighbourhood, for that while she
lived she would remain mistress of her own place,
and that after her own fashion.

Sir Lynam, who had the best reasons in the world
for remaining on good terms with the lady of Starkey,
found this suggestion of hers by no means at variance
with his taste. He bought a cottage some miles
distant, which he set about converting into a little
hunting-lodge ; built a kitchen and out-houses the
size of the building itself, and stables four times as
large as all together ; laid out gardens and shrubberies ;
kept gardeners, grooms, and servants of every descrip-
tion ; hung paintings of all the celebrated hunters and
racers in the three kingdoms on the walls of his din-
ing-room ; fitted up a handsome billiard-room, and
laid down a bowling-green ; built a smoking-house
in his garden ; and according to his taste made it as
complete as possible, leaving no want but that of jolly
companions to fill it.

Jolly companions, however, were not wanting long.
Some came from Hertfordshire, some from London,
and some from the very neighbourhood of Starkey

itself. Lady Thicknisse by no means admired the mob of men, as she called them, who accompanied Sir Lynam to Starkey to eat the shooting luncheons to which she invited him, nor the excesses in which they indulged; she told him so, and he promised not to annoy her again. To promise, with many people, is much more easy than to perform, and so it always was with Sir Lynam. Lady Thicknisse was annoyed more and more; she declared that the peace of her life was at an end; and at a private interview to which she summoned Sir Lynam, informed him solemnly that he never should inherit one inch of the Starkey estate unless he either reformed or removed himself and his fellows from the county. Sir Lynam took alarm, and removed himself not only from the county, but from the island itself, and for seven years Starkey and Lady Thicknisse were in quiet.

Shortly, however, before the time at which this our present story commences, some restless demon or other sent Sir Lynam back to his old hunting-seat, no way improved either in character or manners; and Mrs. Betty's letters of late had been filled with the mad pranks of Sir Lynam, and the misunderstandings between himself and Lady Thicknisse.

"Strange indeed is it," said one of Mrs. Betty's letters, "that Sir Lynam should go on in this way, when he has such a frail hold on Starkey—not being, as I hinted to you in my last, its rightful heir. My sister-in-law makes no longer any secret of this singular affair with me, and I can now give you a clearer idea of it than I was able to do in my last. On the death of the late Sir Sampson, everybody wondered.

as you may remember, how it was that Starkey, as well as the Hertfordshire property, did not go to the heir-at-law—but the reason was this. Lady Thickmisse, in her researches among the old family papers, had found a singular clause in the will of Sir Sampson's great-uncle, the first possessor of Starkey, and the amasser of the family wealth, of which clause I have obtained a copy from Mr. Twisleden. It runs thus:—

" 'And furthermore I devise, that after the third in descent from me the testator, the freehold of Starkey, with its mansion, commonly called Starkey-Hall or Starkey, together with all therein contained of family plate, jewels, and other personal property then existing, left by me, together, with all farms, woods, mines, fisheries, &c., and all rights and appurtenances thereunto belonging, shall descend to the then existing heir or heirs direct, male or female, of my sole sister Joan, with whom I had a quarrel during a game of cribbage, on the twenty-fifth day of December, being Christmas Day, in the year of our Lord 1712, which said Joan, then Merivale, being the wife of John Peter Merivale, cordwainer in the city of London, died in indigence in the parish of Marylebone, London, on or about the 21st of June, in the year of our Lord 1736, leaving two sons and two daughters.'

" The will," said Mrs. Betty, " went on to state many particulars respecting this unfortunate Joan Merivale, who, it seems, had in vain besought reconciliation, and had even came up to Starkey with her children for that purpose; 'when,' says the will, 'in pride and unbrotherly hardness of heart the said testator closed the door in her face, for which, afterwards, when it was too late, he suffered much remorse and penitence, especially when he lost his two eldest children—the one by fire, and the other by water; and that therefore, as some reparation, he willed that the two next generations should merely hold the property of Starkey in trust for the direct descendants of the said Joan Merivale in the third generation; and that in case of there being none such, he the said testator willed that the said property of Starkey be sold by public auction, and the product thereof be placed in the hands of the Admiralty, for the building of ships-of-war.'

"Such being this remarkable clause," said Mrs. Betty, " it is plain enough that this property belongs not by right to Sir Lynam. Whether heirs of this unfortunate Mrs. Merivale exist now I know not, but the late Sir Sampson being in the third generation from the testator, it, in obedience to the will, went into other hands. The will, however, had been clearly forgotten, and but for the researches of Lady Thicknisse herself, would probably never have been looked into again. Such being the case, however, it was evidently the interest of Sir Lynam to keep on the most friendly footing with Lady Thicknisse, who had such a terrible secret in her keeping, and who had thus the means of as completely disinheriting him as if the property were *bona fide* her own, although she had not the power of choosing her own heir; this, of course, being no other than the third in direct descent from this unfortunate Mrs. Merivale.

"Sir Lynam does not believe even to this day that Lady Thicknisse will put in force the will. He cannot believe it, for he has used no means to conciliate her, and only the last week bespoke, from a company of strolling players, the performance of a low-lived play in her name; and thus when she drove out, by mere accident, she had the unspeakable annoyance of seeing great handbills on walls and blacksmiths' shops, announcing that "at the special request of Lady Thicknisse, of Starkey, the favourite play of the Miller and his Three Wives, was to be performed." Nothing could equal her displeasure at this audacious use of her name; and it has, I have no doubt, been a means of determining her to fulfil the wishes of the old Sir Timothy, which, in my humble opinion, I think is no more than what is simply right. She, however, I hear from Mr. Twisleden, has made up her mind, and nothing you know after that can turn her.

"What her exact plans of action in this singular affair will be, I know not. My opinion is, that she will not allow the heir or heirs of Mrs. Merivale to know what fortune is theirs during her own lifetime; and that certainly would be the most prudent, as, though I am by no means learned in such things, it appears to me that she would be liable to vast demands of back-rents and such like, from the time of Sir Sampson's death, now five-and-thirty years since. It is a strange affair, however, and one which, one way or another, occupies almost all Mr. Twisleden's time.

"As I said before," continued Mrs. Betty, "who or what this Joan Merivale's descendants are, I know not; the greatest secrecy is preserved on this subject, although I have every reason to believe that Lady Thicknisse has had her eye upon them for several years."

So far Mrs. Betty Thicknisse, in one of her last letters.

The very morning after the evening which opened this volume, we must see Elizabeth Durant and her mother sitting over their breakfast-table.

" Well, it is the most extraordinary thing in the world !" exclaimed the mother.

" Most strangely extraordinary !" returned Elizabeth, glancing still at the letter which she had just hastily read aloud to her mother. " Most extraordinary !"

" Dear, dear !" said Mrs. Durant, in a tone of vexation, " what a thing it is to be born fortunate ! I wish to heaven it had happened to you—but you are not one of the fortunate sort," added she, with a sigh.

Elizabeth continued to peruse the letter, and her mother sipped her coffee with a countenance of great dissatisfaction. " You might just as well read the letter aloud," said she ; " you know how it vexes me to have any one reading at meals."

Elizabeth made no reply, but immediately read as follows :—

" *Starkey, Oct.* 10, 18—.

" I put aside, my dear god-daughter, a long letter which I began to you some weeks ago, in order to have an entire sheet for the strange news I have to communicate to you and your dear mother.

" Of Sir Lynam's late goings-on I need say little more than that they have been such as they have been for some years past ; whether, however, Lady Thicknisse had any returnings of affection towards

him or not I cannot say, but she took it into her head
last week to put his regard to her to a very singular
test, which itself originated in a very trifling oc-
currence.

" We were all sitting together in the library, Mr.
Twisleden, she, and I, when Jewel—you remember
Jewel, her little pet spaniel—fell into a fit, and seemed
at the point of death ; my sister-in-law, who is greatly
attached to the little animal, took him in her lap,
supported his head, and shed many tears over him.
In half-an-hour he recovered, licked her hand, looked
up in her face, and by all little means in his power
seemed as if he wished to show his affection for her.
The poor little creature had been for long accustomed
to bring out of a certain corner her warm slippers of
an evening, she being troubled with cold feet towards
night. This evening he went as usual to bring them,
but he crawled along with a drooping head, and dim
eyes—it quite affected me ; but what was most singular and affecting of all was, that he laid the slipper
down before her, looked up in her face, licked her
hand, and then died. His last sentiment, if you can
apply that word to an irrational creature, was attachment to his mistress.

" We were all affected extremely.

" ' I tell you what,' said Lady Thicknisse, after
some time, ' yon fellow, Sir Lynam, has not a hun-
dredth part the affection for me of this poor brute ;
he would be glad to know that I was dead—and yet,'
added she, ' I have been like a mother to him.'

" ' Nay, nay,' said Mr. Twisleden, ' I think not so
ill of Sir Lynam as that.'

" ' I wish I thought well of him,' said she. ' The

death of this poor beast,' began she again, 'has touched my heart deeply. Would to God I knew that Sir Lynam loved me—that I knew that he even would shed a tear for my death!'

" ' He is much attached to you,' said Mr. Twisleden—' more attached than you think.'

" ' Heaven forbid !' returned she, ' that I should wrong any one—that I should wrong him, of all men, for I have given him reason to expect great things from me ; and what between my duty, and a lingering affection for this young man, I am neither easy in my mind or in my conscience. But I will try him once more,' said she ; ' and if he love me not, why then I will at once seek for respect and gratitude from strangers.'

" I knew what she meant by these words; but I had no idea of the scheme she would make use of to test Sir Lynam.

" ' You shall ride over, said she, ' to-morrow morning to Sir Lynam. You can look grave enough, said she, with a smile ; ' look your gravest and saddest, and say to him that his worthy relative, Lady Thicknisse, is dead.'

" Mr. Twisleden started, and laid his hand on her arm, as if shocked at the idea.

" ' Yes,' said she, ' I'll have it done. Eulogise me as much as you will ; tell him of my affection for him, and that my last words were of him ; and if he shed but one tear, may God forgive me my many sins, as I will freely and fully forgive him !'

" It was not for me to give my opinion, whatever it might be, on this strange idea. You, who know her, know also how useless opposition would have been ; nevertheless, Mr. Twisleden said much against it, although in the end he was over-persuaded, and promised to do all faithfully.'

"Sir Lynam was at breakfast with three of his friends the next morning, when the old lawyer, with a very grave countenance, presented himself before him.

"'How is the old lady?' asked Sir Lynam, the moment he entered.

"Twisleden sighed, and shook his head.

"'Ah! how?' exclaimed Sir Lynam, putting at the same time brandy in his coffee.

"'She's dead!—I'll bet you any money she's dead!' exclaimed one of his friends.

"'Starkey's your own, old boy!' said another, clapping him on the shoulder.

"'Gentlemen,' said Twisleden, 'be silent. My business is with Sir Lynam, and with him alone.'

"'We are all friends here,' said Sir Lynam.

"'Sir Lynam, then,' said Mr. Twisleden, 'I am the bearer of melancholy tidings. Your worthy kinswoman, Lady Thicknisse, is dead!'

"'Bravo!' exclaimed the three friends, in one voice.

"You're a rare old fellow!' said Sir Lynam, to poor Mr. Twisleden.

"'And her last words were of you!' continued he. 'Affectionate, loving words, which might have wrung tears from a stone; she loved you, Sir Lynam—indeed, Sir Lynam, she loved you very much!'

"'Has she burnt the will?' interrupted Sir Lynam.

"'She left her blessing on you,' continued Twisleden, 'the kindest of blessings; and her prayer was that you would remember the love and tenderness she had shown you as a boy, and that you would—'

"'Has she burnt the will?' interrupted Sir Lynam again.

"'She was a loving friend, although you were unworthy of her,' said Twisleden; 'and all is as you can wish,' added he, venturing on a falsehood, as he declared, because he wished to touch his heart, if possible.

"'The will is destroyed, then?' said he.

"The lawyer nodded assent, and then added, 'She loved you, Sir Lynam—it is my duty to tell you this—loved you like a mother!'

"'Pleasant dreams to the old girl!' exclaimed he, nothing moved; and then ringing the bell, ordered in hot meat and cold, beer, brandy, and ale, 'that the messenger,' as he said, 'of such rare tidings might eat and drink to his heart's content.'

"But Mr. Twisleden could neither eat nor drink—he declared he never was so hurt in all his life before.

"'I am in no temper for meat or wine,' said he.

"'That's no reason why we should fast,' said one of the three friends; so Sir Lynam and they all sat down to eat and drink, and talk over this great good news.

"Mr. Twisleden ordered, therefore, his servant and horses to the inn, and after an hour's rest he rode silently away. The bells were ringing merrily as he went out of the village, and boys and men were piling up a bonfire before Sir Lynam's gate.

"'What means all this rejoicing?' asked he.

"'Sir Lynam has come to a great inheritance!'—'Sir Lynam makes merry because old Lady Thicknisse is dead?' said they.

"Poor Mr. Twisleden told us all this with tears in

his eyes; he declared that Sir Lynam's conduct made his very heart ache.

"All that evening he and Lady Thicknisse spent together in the library. On the next evening she sent for the Rev. Mr. Vesey, ordered in the old steward, and good Mrs. Perigord the housekeeper, of whom you know we have so high an opinion, and in presence of these, having taken an oath of secrecy from them during her pleasure, she made Mr. Twisleden read the will of the old Sir Timothy, which, of course, caused the greatest amazement. Mr. Twisleden made his remarks on the will as he went on; the opinion, he said, of the first lawyer of the day had been taken on it—Sir Lynam was not the rightful heir. 'The rightful heir,' said Lady Thicknisse, taking the words out of his mouth, ' is one on whom my eye has been fixed these several years—a young and beautiful girl. the sole daughter of Thomas Franklin, merchant of the city of London, who was son of the second son of the said Joan Merivale—the eldest son dying unmarried, as did also both daughters; documents in proof of which are in my possession.'"

" You've read enough—you've read enough, child,' said Mrs. Durant, interrupting her daughter, and speaking in a tone of vexation and annoyance.

" Dear Alice!" said Elizabeth, " what a most wonderful change for her! She looks born to be the mistress of Starkey!"

" I think there must be some mistake about it," said Mrs. Durant. " Franklin is by no means an uncommon name; and so strange it is that they should themselves know nothing of this family connection. It must be some other Franklins!"

" No, there's no mistake at all," returned Elizabeth. " Mrs. Betty goes on to say, that it is our own
friend, Alice, the daughter of her old friend—but
shall I not finish the letter?"

" No, no ; I've heard it already," said Mrs. Durant,
" and I do not want to hear it again."

CHAPTER IV.

MORE LETTERS AND MORE NEWS.

AFTER taking the most kindly leave of Maitland
in the glass-coach which conveyed them home, Mrs.
Franklin and her daughter found the card of Mr.
Twisleden, and a note, on the drawing-room table.
The servant said the gentleman who left them was
greatly disappointed at not finding Alice or her mother
at home ; the note said the same thing, but added
that Mr. Twisleden would return again at ten the
next morning, as his visit had reference to most important business. It was altogether a mystery and
an excitement ; the name of Twisleden was unknown
to them, for if they had heard it mentioned, in the
many conversations they had had with Elizabeth and
her mother about Starkey, it had never fixed itself in
their memories. " It must be somebody about the
broken ring," said Alice—" Or somebody about the
shares in the water-company, which were entered in
your name," said her mother—" Or those shares in
the Montgomeryshire canal, which have never yet
paid any dividend," said Mr. Netley.

Everybody speculated, but nobody approached the truth. Eleven hours, however, soon slide on, even though people may lie awake half a night in uncertainty and doubt; and so ten o'clock came in due course of time, and with it Mr. Twisleden, punctual to his engagement.

People are not very incredulous when they are to be convinced of their own good fortune, however unlooked-for it may be, or however strange the channel may be through which it comes; nor if a handsome estate hangs upon it, would any one be extremely angry at its being made as plain as daylight that their great-grandfather was a shoemaker. Both Alice and her mother declared their entire ignorance of the fact; Mr. Thomas Franklin, Alice's father, had been mostly abroad with his merchant-ships; he had said nothing of his grandfather, but his widow and his daughter were quite convinced that it must be as Mr. Twisleden so obligingly asserted. Yes, indeed, it is the most easy and agreeable thing in the world to believe oneself "heir to a great fortune. And yet, after all, it was very strange; strange to have been for so many years a person of so much consequence without ever suspecting it—to have been for so many years an object of interest and attention to a great lady so many miles off, who all the while held in ward for one property to the amount of fifteen thousand a year!" So thought Alice, looking very serene all the time, whilst Mrs. Franklin herself seemed as if she would overwhelm the old gentleman by her civilities.

Mr. Netley, who was naturally given to calculation wherever pounds, shillings, and pence were con-

cerned, and who, while his niece looked through a
sunshiny prospective to her fifteen thousand a year,
took on his part a retrospective glance at five-and-
thirty years of unpaid income—in fact, ever since the
time of the late Sir Sampson's death, and hinted, in
the politest manner possible, something to that purpose. Mr. Twisleden, spite of all his professional
tact, looked momentarily confused, but Alice and her
mother unanimously disclaimed all such thought.
They were at this moment too grateful—too much
penetrated with universal charity, to dream of making
any claim whatever of such a nature ; they wondered
at Mr. Netley with great warmth ; and he, good old
man, like a child reproved for its officiousness, remained submissively silent, whatever his own thoughts
might be.

Alice Franklin received at once into the very
depth of her soul the agreeable and flattering consciousness that she was the undoubted and undis-
puted heiress of Starkey, of which she had heard so
much ; that she was greater even than the great
Lady Thicknisse herself ; that she could command
from this day forth fifteen thousand a year ; that
she was fit to mate with an earl, and, moreover, that
she was young and beautiful—all which combined together were enough to turn a head much wiser, and
to warp a mind much stronger, than Alice Franklin's. Without, however, censuring Alice, we appeal
to thee, gentle reader : was not all this somewhat too
great a trial for any human nature whatever ? But
we will leave that question, and return to Alice.

Whatever her secret feelings might be, and however in the end all this great good-fortune might

E

operate upon her character, nothing could be more graceful and becoming than her demeanour at the present time. She looked her loveliest; she looked like one high-born and high-bred—like one who, far above the station which she had hitherto occupied, would dignify that to which she was now called. Mr. Twisleden, old man as he was, felt himself quite captivated by her; whilst, had he been an archangel descended direct from heaven, he could not have been made more of than he was by them all.

What, during this while, were Alice's feelings towards Henry Maitland? Ah! it is hard to say. She was not a girl who, out of the abundant warmth and generosity of her own heart, had been attached to her lover, not only for his own excellence, but because he was so deeply devoted to her. Alice thought herself superior to most women, and even had she been without expectations from her uncle Netley, she would still have thought that she honoured Maitland in promising him her hand; but now, she felt as much above him as heaven is above earth. Involuntarily she thought of her broken ring, and then, in the natural remembrance of his great affection for her, she wished he had loved her less, because she knew how easy it would be for herself to dissolve the bond between them. Her uncle, too, though he said nothing, thought on the same subject, and said to himself, " I always knew she would never marry poor Maitland ! "

" Alice, my love,"— said her mother to her that night, after they had made hasty preparations to accompany Mr. Twisleden to Starkey the next morning,—" you should leave a note for Henry ; he was

to have gone with us, you know, to the Opera to-morrow
night; it will be such a surprise to him!
Your uncle can take the letter. I wish you could
have seen him before you had gone,—but then, you
know, he can follow us to Starkey."

"Oh, no!" said Alice, coldly and proudly—think-ing,
as it were, aloud.

"You are the mistress of Starkey, my dear," re-turned
her mother. "You have a right to invite
any one there, more especially Henry. Lady Thick-nisse
will like him, my dear."

"Mr. Maitland must wait my pleasure," said
Alice, in an under voice, and then sat down to write
a hasty note, which she intended to be kind, but
which, after all, was cold.

"Well, I declare, after all," said Mrs. Franklin,
as they drove along the North road the next morn-ing,
"you never wrote a note to Elizabeth Durant,
as you said you would. Poor thing! I am afraid she
will take it unkind—and I would not for the world,
Alice," added she, "that you should appear to neglect
your friends."

Alice had been thinking of the omission with regret
herself; "But I really was so occupied yesterday,"
said she, "I had no time for anything. My uncle
Netley will call on her, I am sure; he will want
something to do now we are gone. Poor Elizabeth!"
added she with a sigh, thinking with a feeling akin
to deep compassion on her hopeless industry, which
just kept her above want, and that was all.

Let us turn now for a moment to Henry Maitland.
Had a thunderbolt fallen on him, he could not have
experienced a greater shock than he did on receiving

Alice's note.   It gave him no pleasure, much as he loved her.   Could he himself have endowed her with fifteen thousand a year, he would not have envied the richest monarch in Europe.   As it was, it seemed to him that this rich inheritance at once placed an impassable gulf between them ; and all that the kind old Nehemiah Netley could do, could not remove the load of suspicion and uncertainty from his soul.

Mr. Netley had set out intending to go to Elizabeth Durant's as soon as he had made this call ; but he remained for hours with Henry, and then came in Henry's father, the rich old silversmith.   Very different, indeed, was the effect of this strange news on him.   It was impossible for him to take any other than a golden view of everything ; he saw at once his son as the husband of Alice, the possessor of Starkey, and began to turn over in his mind all kind of schemes and plans for endowing him worthily.   He would make a transfer of funded property to him ; he would make a deed of gift that very day ; he would liberate him from every connexion with trade, excepting in as much as subsequent share of profits would go.   Mr. Henry Maitland the elder was generosity's self ; he had always liked Alice ; he fairly adored her now ; and declared that he would himself make her the present of such a ring as would be worthy the acceptance of the heiress of Starkey.   The idea of any change of feeling on her part never once entered his head.

There is something wonderfully infectious in a cheerful spirit.   Henry could not help being influenced by his father, and he, too, began to indulge in bright and joyous hopes.   The two old gentlemen, therefore, went by themselves to the Opera, and he remained at home, to pour out all his soul in a letter to Alice at Starkey.

The first news which any of the London friends had from Starkey was in a letter from Mrs. Betty to Elizabeth Durant, and was as follows :—

" Starkey, Oct. 27.

" The first calm moments, my dear young friend, which I can command, I dedicate to you, in order that you and your good mother may be duly informed of the painful and distressing event which has just occurred. My sister-in-law is dead—died last evening about six o'clock.

" But in order that you may have a clear idea of this melancholy affair, I will endeavour to give you a detailed account of all that has happened since my last. In my own mind, I must confess that I was not at all satisfied with the trick that was put on Sir Lynam—it seemed to me at the time like a tempting of Providence ; but I did not feel it my place to interfere, because Lady Thicknisse had always been used to her own ways, and took interference ill from any one.

" The report that she was dead spread far and wide, as was but natural, and upon which she never could have calculated, so much annoyed and troubled did she appear by it. She had hoped, no doubt, that Sir Lynam would have evinced some sorrow; she had a hankering, it is my opinion, to be again reconciled with him, and she wished to make this the occasion of it ; but however that in reality might be, she was extremely wounded by his conduct, and got into a very irritable state of mind. Then, too, there was a deal of necessary excitement about making Sir Timothy's will known, although as yet that was only done in her own household, as it were; and although she had all needful documents prepared, and at hand for use whenever she might determine upon taking these decided steps, yet still there was a deal to be done at last; and then, when everything really was ready for Mr. Twisleden to set off on his journey to London, whether she was timid or undecided, or whether she had misgivings, I know not, but certain it was the carriage was ordered out four different times before she would finally consent to Mr. Twisleden going. Poor lady! it had been her intention for many years to retain firm possession of the property till her death; she was now, as it seemed, about to give it out of her hands during her lifetime. It seemed even to me at that time a hazardous step, as far as her own interests went, although I confess that, as a question of right, it was no more than her duty. However, an awful Providence was at work in it all, and whatever He does is best.

"At five o'clock in the evening, just as it was getting dusk, Mr. Twisleden set off post to London; she sat up till twelve—although she had prayers as usual, at ten, and then went to bed. At three, however, she rang her bell violently, and ordered an express to be prepared instantly, to ride for life and death to London after Mr. Twisleden, with a letter, which she must have written during the night. She breakfasted at eight on chocolate, as usual, and seemed tolerably calm; but at eleven she had a sudden apoplectic fit, which affected the whole of one side, and

deprived her of speech.   Dr. Law, who was immediately summoned, was in the utmost alarm, and gave
no hope whatever of her life in case of a second
attack, which he apprehended.   Mr. Vesey was sent
for, and administered the sacrament, which, though
she was quite speechless, she took with apparent com-
fort, which was an unspeakable satisfaction to me.
Dr. Law remained with her during the night.   The
next day she made signs for pen, ink, and paper,
which were given her.   She made inquiries whether
any tidings had been received from Mr. Twisleden.
Poor lady! she had lost all consciousness of time, and
seemed greatly surprised to find he had been gone,
comparatively speaking, but a few hours.   She seemed
very restless and uneasy in her mind, but would communicate nothing either to Mr. Vesey or the physician.   All her thoughts were of Mr. Twisleden and
the express which she had sent after him.   My idea
was that the letter, which she had sent thus, was to
countermand her directions to Mr. Twisleden, and
that she was now uneasy at having done so, which
idea seemed justified by what followed. On the fourth
day she had, in part, recovered her speech; and a
letter arriving that evening from Mr. Twisleden, she
expressed great eagerness to know its contents.   I
steadied her head between my hands to enable her to
read it.   Mr. Twisleden stated that his mission had
been most successful, and that himself and the young
heiress would be at Starkey in a couple of days at
most after the receipt of this. He said nothing of
the letter which she had sent express after him; he
either had not received it, or had not acted upon
it.   Mr. Twisleden's letter seemed to give her great

satisfaction. ' It is all right!' said she; 'all right I shall die in peace.' She then ordered herself to be raised in bed, sent for her house-steward and housekeeper to her bedside, and gave orders to them to get all in readiness for the reception of their new mistress. It was a very affecting thing; her voice was unsteady, and she spoke with difficulty, but her mind was clear and calm; there was, too, a gentleness and a collectedness in her eye, which assured my mind that she was at peace with her own conscience.

" ' Get all things ready,' said she to her servants, ' for this is a greater guest who is now coming than has ever been received since the days of the late Sir Sampson. I shall not be long with you,' said she. ' I am on my way to another mansion, which, I trust, is also prepared for me. Your new mistress is on the way; she, even now, approaches the door. The young and the old have very different ways: things will be changed here—with new masters come new manners; but, my friends,' said she, ' be as faithful to your new mistress as you have been to me—and may God bless you!'

". There was not a dry eye amongst us. The two good old servants kissed her hand, and wept like children. Nobody, of course, made any reply to her; and those were her last words.

" Two hours afterwards she had a second attack; and at three o'clock the next day died—yes, at the very moment when the carriage drove into the court which brought us our new mistress.

" This has been, as you may believe, a great shock to me—but God's will be done

" *October* 29.

" I have been prevented finishing my letter by a slight attack of indisposition ; and now, two days after my former date, I take up my pen to conclude.

" My poor sister-in-law is to be interred next Thursday Miss Franklin, who appears wonderfully collected and clear-headed for so young a person, has ordered the greatest honours to be paid to the remains of her predecessor. We hear that Sir Lynam has given it out that he shall appear as chief mourner—a piece of audacity which surprises me even in him. Miss Franklin—I cannot call her Alice, as I used to do in my letters to you, for her manners even to me, her mother's old friend and your godmother, do not encourage such familiarity.—Miss Franklin, then, seemed at first greatly shocked and affected by the death of my poor sister-in-law. ' It made her arrival at Starkey ill-starred,' she said ; nor will she see the corpse, which, perhaps, is only natural, for the young shrink, as if instinctively, from death and pain.

" It was upwards of forty years since I had seen her mother : we were then young girls at school ; and afterwards, as you have heard, kept up a young lady friendship and correspondence, which lingered on for ten years, and then died a natural death— until some little revived by your acquaintance with her and her daughter through my means. I still see some traces of her early self, especially in the eyes. She looks remarkably well for her years, and is certainly, as you say, very stout.

" Great changes will, no doubt, be made at Starkey, but as yet nothing is said of what kind. Miss Franklin, I dare say, does not at all know yet what she will do. I see very little of her, as she keeps very much in her own room. Her harp is come down, and I have heard a very sweet voice accompanying it. She is very handsome, and seems remarkably well-instructed ; but there is something cold in her manners, which, in one so young, does not quite please me ; but, after all, I find she is not so young as I at first supposed her. I fear, however, that she is too calculating and prudential to be very amiable—but we shall see. Such a mistress as this will make Starkey far and wide renowned.

"My spirits are by no means good at this time. I have many fears and misgivings, I hardly know why. I fear changes of any kind. I am an old woman, and for the remainder of my days I covet rest. It would pain me extremely to leave Starkey. I was born here ; I have lived all my days here ; this place seems a part of myself; and I feel that it would be like sundering mind and body to remove me. For upwards of forty years I have slept in one chamber. I am foolish as a child, for the very knots in the boarded floor, and the very cracks in the window-panes, are to me like old friends. But God's will be done. Man proposes and He disposes ; that has ever been the ordination of things, and it is best.

"Yours ever, my dear god-daughter,

"BETTY THICKNISSE."

"P.S.—I should think there is no doubt but that Miss Franklin will respect the will of her predecessor; for though, perhaps, in the eye of the law, she had no right to will any part, even of her own savings, still I think what few annuities there were she will

continue, though I am distressed to find no mention
in the will of annuities, not even your dear mother's;
and what few legacies and such like she has bequeathed
to old servants, will and ought to be paid."

" What changes will the new mistress of Starkey
make?" said Mrs. Betty, anxiously, to herself; and
" What changes will she make?" asked the alarmed
Mrs. Durant, aloud, to her daughter; " What's to
become of me, for you see the old lady has made no
provision for me—or if Alice should not continue the
annuity?"

" Prosperity mostly makes a young heart generous," said Elizabeth. " I think, besides, that Alice
never would discontinue your annuity. She knows,
as well as we do, how important it is to you."

" And you remember her wish the other night,"
said Mr. Netley, who had entered unperceived, and
who had heard her last words. " You remember how
she wished it might be in her power to benefit you."

Mr. Netley had heard of Lady Thicknisse's death,
and he brought now a newspaper with him, containing
an account of this " Immense and Unexpected Inheritance," as it was headed.

" Neither I nor Henry Maitland have yet heard
from her," said the old gentleman. " My niece
Franklin wrote on their arrival. I want Henry to
go down there next week."

" And you," said Elizabeth, " will not you go too?"

" No, no," returned he, " I shall wait and see how
she goes on; prosperity tries people more than adversity; and if she don't please me I shall never go
near her."

CHAPTER V.

A PATERNAL SCHEME FRUSTRATED.

Long before this extraordinary case of " Immense and Unexpected Inheritance" had been spread by the newspapers through the length and breadth of England, it reached the ears of the old lawyer, Sir Thomas Durant ; and no sooner had he become acquainted with it, than he thought his own thoughts on it, and schemed his own schemes.

But before we make known the old lawyer's speculations, we must introduce to our readers his son Philip, in the midst of his little household.

Sir Thomas and his son were of very opposite characters, besides which, the former was one of those fathers whose affection seems to cool towards their sons as they approach manhood. Perhaps they fear in them a sort of rival, or perhaps, having no longer the same influence and mastery over them as when they were boys, they regard them as insurgents, who, to be kept in order, must be kept under with the strong arm of power. However that might be, Sir Thomas, who had doted on his son as the apple of his eye in childhood, had now to all appearance not only cast him off to fate, but had steeled his heart stedfastly against him ; whilst all this time one of the most striking characteristics of the son was the most remarkable attachment to his father. Blind to his faults he certainly was not, but his affection for him was almost an instinctive passion. The disunion with his father hung like a cloud over his existence.

One of the crowning offences of the son had been the befriending the incendiary, Richard Durant. One misunderstanding grew upon another, and at last widened to what appeared an irreconcileable breach ; and, subsequently, after several unhappy months of discord, Philip left his father's house, determined to commence his own professional career untrammelled, and, if possible, unoffendingly, and take whatever opportunities offered of reconciliation. Months, however, upon months went on, and Sir Thomas, offended by his son's independence, which to him looked like defiance, seemed more than ever to set his face against him.

Philip, as we have seen, in the meantime married ; it was the most unwise step he could have taken, as Elizabeth's mother had said over and over again, more particularly as, whatever other qualities the young wife might boast of, she had neither fortune nor connexions to recommend her.

Philip Durant was not worldly-wise, and in marrying he must have done it either uncounting of consequences or in defiance of them. Still, as yet, although he had carefully kept his marriage from the knowledge of his father, he had not repented of it. Reconciliation with his father, it seemed to him, would make his earthly felicity complete ; and the more he kissed his own infant son, the more did his heart warm towards his own parent.

Gertrude, Philip's young wife, was sitting one morning beside her sleeping child, when her husband entered the room.

" You look happy, dearest," said she ; " you must be the bearer of good news."

" A note from my father," said he, " bids me come to him this evening ; this is the first step he has himself made. I cannot help prognosticating good."

" Ah ! if he will but be kind to us—if he will but let me love him." said she. " I never knew my own father ; but I could love yours with all the affection of a daughter ; and this sweet child of ours—" said she, lifting the light covering from his face : " Is your father fond of children, Philip ? "

Philip stooped down and kissed his boy ; he remembered when he had been a little child, and had sat on his father's knees, and the thought filled his eyes with tears.

" Sharple brought the note to me," said he, after a pause, " and said that now was the true time for reconciliation. I never liked the man," said he, " never believed him my friend ; but my father has not hitherto made any advances, and I augur well from this."

" Perhaps he feels his health decline," said Gertrude. " Affection which has been cool in middle life often revives with age or infirmity. Oh, how happy we would make your father, would he but let us ! I would so patiently bear any ill-humour from him ; I would indulge all his whims ; I would sing to him, I would play to him—you say he is fond of music. I would teach my boy to love him," continued she, affection lighting up her whole being ; " I would teach him to sooth him—to win his very soul from him, as children only can ! Oh, Philip, how we will all love that dear old man, and how happy we will make him!"

Philip kissed his wife, and, filled with happy hopes, hastened to his father as soon as the day began to darken.

Sir Thomas sat in his dingy old room, among his old law-books and papers as he had done years before, when his son entered.

"We'll let bygones be bygones," said the father, returning the pressure of his son's hand somewhat warmly. "I want to speak to you now with regard to the future."

Philip seated himself, and awaited, not without anxiety, his father's words.

"You have heard," said he, "of the inheritance which has so unexpectedly come to the daughter of Mrs. Franklin—to your cousin Alice?"

Philip replied in the affirmative.

"You had some little fancy for her some years ago," said the father; "perhaps have so, even yet."

"Miss Franklin is a very handsome girl," remarked Philip, no little alarmed at the tendency of his father's words.

"That's cool," said Sir Thomas; "but look you, Philip, it is my will and pleasure that you marry this same Alice Franklin."

"I know what Starkey is," continued he, seeing his son indisposed to answer. "Mrs. Franklin will make no objection to the match; you are good-looking enough, and on good terms, I make no doubt, with them all. I can make the match worth even the attention of the lady of Starkey."

" This is what you have to propose to me ? " said
Philip.

" On these conditions," returned the father, " I
will overlook what is past.   You hesitate ; you are
low in the world, Philip ; you want money ; that
shall matter nothing, I will provide for you amply."

" I cannot comply with your conditions," returned
Philip ; " I cannot marry Alice Franklin."

" Cannot ! " repeated his father. " I say you shall.
Maybe," added he after a moment's pause, " you
have some foolish love-affair in hand.   This is not
the age of romance, Philip ; every one looks to
himself.   In a month's time Alice Franklin will
be beset with suitors.   Come, now, be wise : you
have won both the mother and daughter by all your
fine notions of honour and integrity ; your very
quarrel with me, and the occasion of it, made
them think all the better of you.   I am getting old,
Philip," said he in a milder voice.   " I have laid out
plans for my old age.   I will re-build Stanton
Combe—Starkey is a fine estate.   There has been
disunion long enough between us."

Philip covered his face with his hands, for his
father's words had touched him deeply.

" I did not think, Philip," said the old lawyer,
" that you would have needed all this.   I thought
you loved me."

" Alice is engaged to another," at length said he,
glad to find an impediment, and not strong enough
at that moment to avow the truth as regarded himself.

" Engaged, is she ? " returned Sir Thomas, with a
sneer.   " The Alice Franklin of yesterday," said he,

" is not the Alice Franklin of to-day ; the heiress of Starkey will have other views in marriage than the heiress of old Netley of Ludgate-hill! But," said he, dropping his voice into a whisper which had something fearful in it, " perhaps the impediment lies in yourself; perhaps the sister of Richard Durant.—"

" No," said Philip ; " no such engagement exists, or ever has existed, between me and Elizabeth Durant."

" Good !" returned his father. " I believe you ; those words have the tone of truth in them : and I'll tell you what, Philip ; I know how poor, how miserably poor, are the Durants. Do you marry the heiress of Starkey, and I will take care of the Durants myself. On my word,—and I never forfeited my word,—I will settle two hundred a-year on mother and daughter, and all prosecution of the son shall cease. Bygones shall be bygones !"

Poor Philip ! he walked up and down the room in fearful communion with himself. Then was the time, if such a time were ever to come, in which he was to repent of his marriage. He saw in quick mental vision things as they might have been ; the beautiful Alice Franklin as his wife, and himself as the possessor both of Starkey and Stanton Combe ; he saw speedy reconciliation with his father, and ease and worldly prosperity around him. On the other hand, and what was it? a dreaded secret to be unfolded—his father's wrath—his curse perhaps, which would strike him down from the verge of union on which he now stood. He glanced at his father, and saw his gray hair and his thin cheek, and a tide of affection, such as he had never felt before, rushed over his soul towards him. O that he might have thrown himself at his feet, have craved his forgiveness, and have annulled the past! So reasoned the weaker part of his nature. Then he thought on the love, the beauty, the patience, the goodness of Gertrude—of what she had hitherto been to him—of what she would yet be ; he thought of her with her mild, angelic beauty—the mother of his boy ; he thought of her in the midst of poverty, and then he thought of Alice Franklin and Starkey ; and his warm, affectionate heart clung to his wife.

"Father," said Philip, re-seating himself, and speaking in a clear, low voice, " I am married ; I am not only married, but I am a father."

Sir Thomas looked as if he did not credit his senses.

"Yes," said Philip, " what I tell you is true. I am married. Be a father to us, to me, to my wife, and my boy ! God in heaven knows," said he, " how earnestly I have longed for reconciliation with you, and for your blessing ! Refuse it not to us ! Let me bring my wife and child to you, let us kneel down before you and receive your blessing ! You are getting old, father ; let us love you—let us make your home rich in love—let us gather about your old age affection and joy."

" Married, are you ?" returned Sir Thomas, in a voice of concentrated displeasure ; " I tell you, then, I will not see your wife. As you have brewed so you may bake ; and further than this, I tell you that I will not exchange a word with you. You may starve ; you may die—you and yours, and I will not waste thought upon you."

" Father !" exclaimed Philip.

"I have nothing more to say," interrupted Sir Thomas, rising, and pale with passion; "not a word Henceforth you and I have nothing in common;" and with these words he left the room.

Philip sat he knew not how long in that room. A throng of agitating feelings rushed through his bosom. He knew his father too well to hope for reconciliation now, if at all; yet, strange as it may seem, never did he court it so much as then. Never had he felt before how capable his heart was of affection towards his parent, and how strong his affection really was. The human heart lives through a long experience in but a short space of time. Philip Durant seemed then most emphatically to learn all that man owes to man in every relationship of life; what parent owes to child, what child to parent, and what husband and wife are to each other. It was a baptism of affection and agony, which called forth and strengthened every human sentiment in his soul.

The sound of his father's heavy coach drawing up to the door recalled him to himself.

Sir Thomas and his son passed from the house at the same moment, without exchanging a word; the one entered his carriage, the other walked slowly homeward.

"Drive on for a quarter of an hour," said Sir Thomas to the footman who waited at the steps for directions.

"Which way?" asked the man.

"No, drive first to Doctors' Commons," said Sir Thomas.

"What mad prank has your father been playing?" asked Nehemiah Netley of Philip the next morning, as he entered his chambers with the morning paper in his hand. "Of all fools," said he, "there are none like old ones!" and, laying the paper before him, he pointed to a particular paragraph.

Philip read, but not aloud: "ROMANCE IN REAL LIFE.—A most extraordinary marriage took place last night, about eight o'clock, the particulars of which, as nearly as can be gathered from report, are as follows:—

"Sir T— D—t, a lawyer of the oldest standing and reputation, and who, according to the opinion of gentlemen of the long robe, is not very far from the bench itself, having had a misunderstanding with his son, who, as report says, has married without the consent of his father, resolved likewise to take unto himself a wife, and that without consent of the son. Accordingly, having possessed himself of a special license, he ordered his coachman to drive along the streets of London for half an hour, by his watch, and then to stop at the corner of the first street which presented itself, and which happened to be ——. Here the learned gentleman alighted, having made a vow, as he afterwards declared, to marry the first woman he met who would take a husband on such conditions. We presume some little discrimination was used, however, on the occasion; for the young lady to whom ' the question was thus abruptly popped,' is, we hear, very pretty—one Mary-Ann Jones, barmaid at the Golden-Cross tavern, in —— street. The young lady in question having listened to the learned gentleman, and finding no objection to a husband with a baronet's title, and no small wealth into the bargain, consented, nothing loth. The happy pair adjourned therefore to the carriage, which was in waiting, and being driven to the Golden-Cross tavern, were united by the clergyman of St. ——, who was sent for on the occasion, and who received, we hear, no small fee for his services.

" The happy bridegroom is, we understand, eighty-two, and the blooming bride eighteen." *

Poor Philip felt sick at heart as he read the vulgar slang of this astounding paragraph. In the agony of the moment he thought of New Zealand, Van Diemen's Land, and the wilds of America, with intense longing.

" Oh that I, and Gertrude, and the child were there !—were anywhere but here, to be a laughing-stock to the vulgar,—to be crushed, and punished, and humiliated thus, by one that we would have died for !" said he, with an aching heart.

---

* A marriage contracted under precisely these circumstances occurred about forty years ago in London. The author does not recollect the name of the gentleman ; the girl he married, however, was one Sarah Becket, a barmaid at a tavern in the City. Her mother was well known to the author, and lived in an almshouse at Uttoxeter. The marriage, as would be most probable, was an unhappy one. The wife's conduct was bad, and after a year or two she was separated from her husband, on a small annuity. The author has frequently seen her when on a visit to her mother, to whom she was kind : she was then near forty, a stout, showy woman, the very personification of tawdry vulgarity.

CHAPTER VI.

TWO RIVAL LOVERS AND AN ACHING HEART.

As a sudden and violent shock will at once restore a drunkard to his sober senses, so did the actual state of affairs at Starkey operate on the prodigal Sir Lynam Thicknisse. His first sentiment, perhaps, was indignation at the trick which had been put upon him; and most desperate were the vows of vengeance he uttered upon the agent of this trick, poor old Mr. Twisleden. To the surprise of his friends, however, this spirit of resentment died away after the first ebullition, and then he sunk into what appeared sullen quiescence.

His jolly friends rallied him; jeered him; tried to make him think light of what had happened; poured out wine for him; rattled the dice in his ears; sung, laughed, and talked; but Sir Lynam remained sad and serious. He who had never been thoughtful before, pondered deeply now, and the more he thought, the more changed were the views he took of all that surrounded him,—nay, even of himself; new objects of ambition started up before him—new desires were created in him.

Sir Lynam, however he had acted the part of a prodigal, was no fool, nor was he one infirm of purpose; he thought and thought, and for three whole days, apart from his friends, took council with himself and determined his plans of action.

On the day before that fixed upon for the interment of the late Lady Thicknisse, therefore, he invited all his friends to dine with him ; and the greatest rejoicing was occasioned among them in consequence, for all naturally supposed that he had overcome his vexation, and was now about to drown its memory in wine.

There never had been a more sumptuous dinner provided in that hunting-lodge than on that day, and at six o'clock Sir Lynam sat down with his friends, not one of whom was not instantly struck and silenced by the grave, determined countenance of the host.

" But he is a wag," said they; " he has some merry prank in his head, which is only to come forth all the brighter for this show of solemnity."

Sir Lynam ate with his guests and pledged them— but that sparingly, and spite of the efforts of every one to be gay, the dinner was as sad as a funeral feast.

After dinner, when the attendants were gone, and he was left alone with his friends, he thus addressed them :—

" The Sir Lynam Thicknisse," said he, " whom you all knew, is dead ; this is his funeral dinner. His heir now stands among you, and asks you to pledge his memory." The glasses were all filled, and the speaker continued. " The late Sir Lynam, like all men, had no doubt his virtues, but his faults and his follies far outweighed them ; the second Sir Lynam, like a wise man, will take warning by the faults of his predecessor,—he will retrieve them, he will be his counterpart ! Gentlemen, you all knew Sir Lynam the first — perhaps you loved him. He gambled, he drank, he spent freely, he lived only for the present

hour, and so that that was gay he troubled himself
no farther.   Gentlemen, Sir Lynam the first had
bad councillors—had reckless, profligate associates;
they drank his wine, they spent his money, they
made him lose a goodly inheritance.   Sir Lynam the
second is wiser than his predecessor.   He will none
of these !   He will spare where the other spent ; he
will drink water where the other drank wine ; he will
go to church where the other went to the tavern !   The
friends of the first Sir Lynam can be none of his !
Gentlemen, let us drink to his memory."

The glasses were emptied, emptied in silence—for
all were offended and confounded, and knew not what
to say ; and after a pause Sir Lynam again spoke.

"Gentlemen, the present Sir Lynam is no more
the past than to-day is yesterday.   In the name of
the late Sir Lynam, I thank you for your friendship
to him—my way of life will henceforth be changed,
and I need you not ; I have taken council with
myself, and I find that I need you not !

" It is inhospitable to dismiss a guest before he
is ready to depart ; it is likewise a breach of good
manners for a guest to stay when the host is weary
of him.   A good-night to you therefore, gentlemen,
and a pleasant journey, whenever you may depart !
For myself, I go to Starkey to-morrow, to attend the
funeral of the late Lady Thicknisse ;" and with these
words, and a low bow, Sir Lynam left the room.

If there had been profound silence during his presence, a clamour of tongues succeeded his departure.
That he was in the most resolute earnest, admitted
not of a doubt ; but how strange was this conduct !—
this abrupt dismissal of them—how unlike him-

self! The gay, reckless, random Sir Lynam, how
was he changed! All were disappointed, all were
in despair—for there was not one of them who could
afford to lose a lavish patron like him. How inhospitable, how ungentlemanly, how queer it was!
The butler, the valet, and many another servant too,
was summoned—and " Is Sir Lynam mad, or is he
drunk, or is this some trick of his?" were questions
which assailed them; but the butler and the valet,
and every domestic about the place, had his grievance
to complain of too—for all had received their dis-
charge. The groom told that the hunters were to
be sold; the butler that the wine must be going to be
sold too, for that Sir Lynam had himself taken count
of every bottle; the valet said that a suit of the
deepest mourning had come home for his master, and
that he would not look even at the new suits which
had just come down from London two days before.
The lodge, they said, was to be shut up, and they
had a notion that Sir Lynam was going to live at the
parson's.

" God in heaven!" exclaimed the friends, and
drank deeply that night at least, to indemnify themselves for the future.

Sir Lynam Thicknisse, in his carriage, followed
the hearse of his deceased relative as chief mourner,
and the day after he besought permission to pay his
respects to the new lady of Starkey.

Alice had heard for years of the wild Sir Lynam,
and knew of his last act of disregard and disrespect
to her predecessor; great, therefore, was her surprise
at his appearance at the funeral—greater still at
his intrusion on her privacy, as she now felt his visit

G

to be. She pictured him in her own mind a rude,
lawless, profligate, who was capable of every incivi-
lity, and perhaps indecorum, even to her. Nevertheless she was curious to see him, so gathering her
mother, Mrs. Betty, and Mr. Twisleden, as a sort of
body-guard about her, she allowed the late heir-
expectant to present himself before her. She had
fancied him in person a blustering, red-faced, ne'er-
do-weel, disreputable-looking person, whom it was
a sort of discredit to be seen with; how great then
was her surprise to see before her a remarkably handsome, slender young man, with a low, prepossessing
voice, and an expression of the deepest melancholy
in his countenance, which, together with his mourning dress, and the air of almost timidity with which
he approached her, as if awed by her presence,—to
say nothing of the peculiar circumstances under
which he presented himself before her,—sent a thrill
to her heart, and an involuntary tear to her eye.

Alice's imagination was instantly excited; her
romantic feelings were interested. This then was the
person into whose inheritance she had so singularly
stepped—who had been, as it were, disinherited by
her! She felt someway as if she had injured him;
she was sorry for him; she wished to set him at ease
with her, to gratify him in some way or other, to
interest him in herself, to make him think her not
unworthy of her fortune; she even wished to gain
some influence over him. She did not, in short,
know what exactly were her definite feelings regarding him; but, at all events, she never had been more
charming than she was then.

A day or two afterwards he made a second call,

and that with many apologies for his want of ceremony, in the evening too. Alice graciously accepted
every apology, and bade him welcome—in truth, she
was glad to see him. They all sat together like a
family party. Sir Lynam was perfectly delightful,
so much of the gentleman: then, he had travelled so
much, and could be really quite entertaining. The
display of his accomplishments piqued her into exhi-
biting hers in return. She sat down to her harp, and
Oh, how bewitching could not Alice look at her harp!
She found that lofty room suited her voice; she
thought, at the same moment, that she was mistress
of that room and of all Starkey, that she was beautiful, and that Sir Lynam was gazing on her with eyes
of unspeakable admiration; and she sang with a consciousness of power which electrified even herself.

Whilst she was singing, however, she thought on
Henry Maitland, for this was his favourite song.
"Well, well!" were her second thoughts: "what
of him at this moment? the past and the future are
alike indistinct; but for the present—I know what is
my object at this moment—I must and will gain an
influence over this man—he *shall* love me, come
what will."

"Good, good!" said the crafty Sir Lynam to himself, as he returned that night to the Thicknisse
Arms, where two rooms were always reserved for his
accommodation. "All will go on right. I know what
I am about. Had she been as ugly as sin I would have
married her: as she is,—lucky Sir Lynam!"

"My dear child," said her mother, some few
weeks afterwards, as they two were sitting together,
" Sir Lynam has just now passed the gates. I bid

you beware of what you are about with regard to that gentleman. Don't forget the old song—'to be off with the old love before you begin with a new.'"

Alice sighed, but all the while was arranging her beautiful hair before a mirror.

"You must not forget, my dear girl, your engagement with Henry," continued her mother. "He is an excellent young man, and most warmly attached to you."

"I know what I am about," returned Alice, wishing all the while in the depth of her own heart that she had fairly done with the old love, to whom she was beginning to be quite indifferent. Her thoughts were something like this: "I never did thoroughly love him, and I ought not to have bound myself to him. How strange it was about the ring! I knew well enough that I never was to have him. Poor fellow! though; I wish he could only be as indifferent to me as I to him!" She then thought of her uncle Netley, and what he would say if she broke with Maitland—she thought of Elizabeth Durant, and what she would think too.

New circumstances alter in many cases our estimate not only of people and things, but of right and wrong also. It was thus with Alice: she thought of her uncle Netley, and of her friend Elizabeth Durant, and of what they would say supposing she were faithless to her former lover, and she felt at that moment almost indifferent to their opinion—or "at least," thought she, "their opinion would very little matter to me in the end. I only wish, however, that poor Henry would transfer his affection to Elizabeth Durant."

"My dear, you should write to Elizabeth Durant," said her mother, just as if her thoughts had been following the course of her daughter's; "she will think it very unkind of you to neglect her thus; and do tell her that you will continue her mother's annuity during her life."

"Yes, that I will," said Alice; "but don't you think I should make it a hundred? I can so well afford it—and poor Elizabeth! she is to be pitied!"

Mrs. Franklin seconded her daughter's suggestion warmly. "I am glad, my love, that you have thought of that; for though a hundred a year is a mere nothing to call an income, yet to those who have hitherto only had fifty, it *is* a nice thing. I hope you will write immediately."

"I will," said Alice; "very soon I will: and I will get Mrs. Betty, who told me to-day that she had a letter to Elizabeth in hand, to make their minds easy about it."

"Sir Lynam Thicknisse is here," said a servant.

"Show him into the library," said Alice, slightly blushing: "see that we have a good fire; and let us have chocolate in as well as coffee."

Mrs. Franklin wondered silently to herself why her daughter ordered in chocolate; she did not remember, as Alice had done, that Sir Lynam a few evenings before had spoken accidentally of his preference for chocolate.

"I have got a letter from my niece Franklin," said Nehemiah Netley to Henry Maitland, a few days after this; "she tells me what a sensation her daughter is creating in the neighbourhood. Old Lady Thicknisse seems in a fair way of being forgotten amongst them. She tells me, too, what a fine place Starkey is, and that Alice has already appropriated a room for me when I visit her. She tells me, too, **that Sir** Lynam is mighty civil and agreeable. Alice had fancied him a sort of bluebeard monster, and he turns out to be an Adonis. I advise you to go and look after your affairs up in the North, **my friend,** else you'll, maybe, lose your mistress."

Maitland had waited for permission from Alice **to** visit her. It was now a month since she had left, and he had received but one letter from her, and that was cold and hurried : she complained of having so much to do and to think of, so much to arrange and so much to inquire into, that she had no time to write more ; and he, who wished to believe her true—who was willing even to deceive himself—waited with the humility—we say nothing of the patience—of the deepest devotion, in **the vain** hope that the day would come when she might have time to spare for him.

" I have not common patience with you, Maitland," said old Netley, a week later ; " you'll get no **per-mission** from her to go to Starkey. **If** she is not **worth looking** after, why, give her **up** at once ! "

Maitland **took the** coach accordingly, and in somewhat more than twelve hours reached the county **of** Durham.

What a thousand pities it is that a worthy, upright man cannot build up self-confidence on the conscious-ness of his own worth and integrity ! **that** he cannot feel—as all assuredly, in another state of being, must come to experience—that nobility **of** mind is before nobility of birth, and that a pure, upright heart is **of** more intrinsic value than the richest rent-roll.

Never did human being moralise more in this strain than did poor Maitland, as he neared Starkey. At last, thought he, what does all my philosophising and moralising signify? I am nothing but the son of a gold-and-silversmith, who, though he is reckoned passingly rich, and most respectable in his ward, is, after all, nothing more than a shopkeeper—what, then, am I in comparison with Alice, the mistress of Starkey and its fifteen thousand a-year? It was a humiliating thought. There was a deal of talk among the coach-passengers about the new lady of Starkey, as they approached her neighbourhood. She seemed to have excited the most intense interest, and to have created a universal sentiment in her favour. Her beauty and her prepossessing manners were warmly extolled; and the liveliest fear was expressed with regard to Sir Lynam Thicknisse's influence over her.

"Ah! see, there is Starkey Hall," said an old Durham gentleman to his neighbour; "no, now it is hid from view: you will see it again at the next opening."

Maitland, who, though so intensely and painfully interested, had taken no part in the conversation, looked out with almost a sickening feeling for the next opening. Anon, and there stood the old, proud Hall of Starkey before him. He heard not the remarks of those around him; he involuntarily closed his eyes, and felt as if he were crushed down into nothingness.

Never had he loved so madly, so blindly, as since he had lost some degree of hope: it was not for her wealth that he loved her, but for her own precious self. "Would to Heaven," said he, "that she were

a beggar on the highway—that she were penniless
and homeless, that I might then prove the reality of
my affection for her! Ten thousand times rather
would I take her as she was, the niece of good old
Netley, than as the mistress of this proud place!"

Once the idea occurred to him of presenting himself before her, and releasing her at once from her
promise to him. But then came the terrible idea—
suppose she accepted his release ; and, Oh, how blank
—how barren—how desolate would not life be to him
without her! He was not heroic enough—or rather,
perhaps, he was not disinterested enough—to risk his
happiness on such a throw ; and who can blame him ?

" No," said he, in that passionate self-communion ;
" faint heart never deserved fair lady ! I will assert
my own right to her boldly—I will win her if I have
the power; and when she is mine—loving her for her
own sake as I do—how I will devote myself to making
her live happy ! Not an angel out of heaven shall
be happier than I will make her, if a love stronger
than death can do anything."

Strengthened by a more worthy self-estimate, and
with a heart made lighter by the most generous and
disinterested affection, Henry Maitland stood before
Starkey on that very evening when Alice, her mother,
and Sir Lynam were drinking chocolate together.

Sir Lynam was taking a volume of the Topography
of Hertfordshire from the shelves as the large New-
foundland dog, and the mastiff, and the hound began
to bark in chorus, as Maitland approached the principal entrance.

" And this," said Sir Lynam, leaning down over the
back of the sofa on which Alice sat, and presenting the

book open before her; "this is the view of my house in Hertfordshire; this is the south front—the avenue, which is here just indicated, is a quarter of a mile long."

"It is a fine old place," said Alice, turning the book to her mother, who was sitting beside her.

"The house is larger than this of Starkey, although the estate is less. It is pure Elizabethan—you would greatly admire it."

"There is so much detail in these old Elizabethan edifices," said Alice, again looking at the plate.

"A gentleman is here," said a servant, presenting a card at the same moment.

"Mr. Maitland," said Alice, in a low voice, her countenance undergoing a change, and her heart beating, but not with pleasure.

"Dear me, Mr. Maitland!" repeated her mother, in that low, quiet tone which expresses anything but welcome; "but he must not be kept waiting, Alice. Do bring him," said she to the servant.

The moment after Maitland entered. To fly to her—to clasp her to his heart—was his first impulse, spite of the imposing influence of place and circumstance; for within a room's space of Alice he forgot that she was mistress of Starkey, and he but a tradesman's son. Something, however, far more depressing and repelling than wealth and station, had he felt these ever so painfully, prevented him from doing more than offering his hand when they met—and that was in Alice herself. It was a miserable meeting!

"And how are you, Mr. Maitland, and how are our London friends? how are my uncle and Eliza-

beth Durant ?" asked she, after a moment of awkward silence.

" Oh! for Heaven's sake," he would have said,
" speak not to me of other people, and above all
things, speak not with that voice !" but he said it
not ; he answered her calmly of that which she asked
for. Sir Lynam stood by her side, as if he had a
right to be there, and though he said nothing, he
stared on Maitland as if he wondered what he had
come for ; and all that time she said not one word to
set him at his ease—to make him feel as if he were
welcome. Never may true lover feel as poor Maitland felt then !

About a week after this time Elizabeth received
the following letter from Mrs. Betty Thicknisse.

" *Starkey, November the 15th.*

" MY DEAR YOUNG FRIEND,—Nothing within the
last half-century has created such a sensation in this
part of the country as these late events at Starkey.

" Miss Franklin, no doubt, has written to you of
her way of life here, but still she is too much occupied
to be a good correspondent ; therefore I shall tell you
all which I think can interest you, without troubling
myself as to whether you have heard of it before or
no. Besides this, I think Miss Franklin, as yet,
knows not what she is about, or what is going on
around her. As yet she is like a person who has
suddenly been hurried up to a vast eminence, and is
then told to look around and comprehend everything ;
she is out of breath, she neither knows this nor that—
where she is, nor whether she stands upon firm ground

or not. I all this while am like a dweller on the hill-top, who, from long observation, and long acquaintance with the land all round, can say where lies this point and where that—on which side lies a precipice, and where a morass—and more than that, who by looking merely on cloud or mist, or even sunshine itself, can say what indicates fair weather and what storm. Thus I look on what is passing around me, and without venturing to do more than whisper now and then a warning word, think to myself my own thought, and tremble—not for myself, but for one so young, so fair, so inexperienced, so tempted, and—pardon me, Elizabeth—so faulty as your friend.

" Miss Franklin is a young person to please, nay almost to fascinate, at first sight : she is the fashion—nay, the very rage here, and every day adds to the crowd of her worshippers. All this however is but natural ; for so many are striving to win her, from interested motives. Starkey never, even in my brother's lifetime, was so much visited as it is now. My poor sister-in-law is already forgot. You will, however, be pleased to know, that her will will in every instance be literally fulfilled ; the old servants have their choice of remaining in their situations or of retiring, and all legacies will be paid. Mr. Twisleden is her councillor as much as he was that of his late mistress ; it is therefore his interest to advise the fulfilment of the will, he is himself so large a legatee. But Twisleden is an honest and good man, and an excellent man of business He is as much captivated by his new mistress as any of the rest, and, which no little surprises, and

I must say displeases me, Miss Franklin, in the absence of her other worshippers, allows herself to seem flattered and gratified by the attentions of poor old Twisleden.

" I myself receive a legacy of six thousand pounds, which together with my own two thousand will amply provide for me, even if I have to leave. As yet I suppose I ought not to expect such a thing, for it has been intimated to me that the house is large enough for us all, and that it is Miss Franklin's pleasure that I should consider it as my fixed home.

" I thought before she came that Mrs. Franklin and I should spend much time together ; but forty years makes a surprising difference in character. Mrs. Franklin, as is quite natural, prefers her daughter's company to mine ; and it is much better—in fact, it is only right that Miss Franklin should always have the countenance of her mother in her really trying, although flattering circumstances.

" You have heard, no doubt, of the singular conduct of Sir Lynam : he is laying violent siege to the heart of the heiress. Had he conducted himself in poor Lady Thicknisse's lifetime as he does now, he never would have lost Starkey. He is a wonder even to me, who know him so well. To see him now, one would imagine he had always been the most regular liver—the most accomplished of fine scholars. Oh, it is absurd to me to see him turning over books of elegant literature, and giving his sentiments on such subjects, and on painting and the fine arts, as if all his days he had been devoted to these things ; and it is no use my saying anything, for both she and her mother seem willing to be duped. His design I clearly enough understand, he is determined to get back Starkey. Whether he will succeed or not, God knows! Did I not, however, know his real character too well to believe this reformation anything but artifice, a means to gain an end, I should think well, even of a spendthrift and prodigal who had self-command and power of resolve enough to reform himself thus, but—However, Miss Franklin will not throw herself away unadvised: there are too many striving for the prize to let any one carry it off easily, and Sir Lynam is not a popular man in these parts.

" *Nov.* 20.—So far I had written, my dear god-daughter, last week. I now take up my pen again, to pursue my little narrative, and, if possible, to finish my letter.

" Last week a lover from London made his appearance, Mr. Henry Maitland—he is acquainted with you, and I had great pleasure in talking of you with him. This young man was, of course, quite a stranger to me, but I was greatly prepossessed in him from the first moment ; and after-observation has interested me still more. What a difference between him and Sir Lynam ! The two both lodged at the inn in the village, and I must confess that, while Mr. Maitland stayed, I was not without anxiety as to what might take place between the two ; but Sir Lynam is a late riser, and I believe, that excepting here, they never met.

" I am an old woman, Elizabeth, and I never thought I should, at my time of life, have been as much interested in any young gentleman as I have been in him.

M

"Mrs. Franklin herself, in a fit of unusual confidence, told me the whole affair. They are ashamed of the son of a London tradesman now, so they want to get rid of him : the daughter takes the same view of the affair as the mother. These most warmly-attached lovers, Elizabeth, are most inconvenient things : they cannot be shaken off like a winter garment ; and now, after I have been consulted and counselled with, and they have endeavoured in vain to make a partisan of me, it has occasioned a coldness between us, which, though I regret, I cannot prevent, for if people will solicit my opinion, they must take it as they find it. I can very well understand their mode of reasoning : this Mr. Maitland, although gentlemanly looking, and most gentlemanly too in his manners, and, by their own showing, disconnected with trade in consequence of this engagement with Miss Franklin, still is only the son of a tradesman, and they are looking much higher than that now. He is, therefore, a most undesirable and inconvenient person, and must be got rid of one way or another. I know nothing, however, of what their views are further ; whether they are satisfied with Sir Lynam, or whether they may be aspiring higher. I will tell you, however, the style of Mrs. Franklin's reasoning, with regard to Mr. Maitland. 'It never will do,' says she, 'to have this thing talked of—we must have an end put to it as quietly as possible—for otherwise it may be of serious disadvantage to Alice. I grant you that he is most blindly and passionately in love ; but then, he ought himself to see exactly what is the state of the case ; and it is not generous, I must say, to hold her to her promise, for the engagement, do you see, was entered into under such different circumstances. Alice is not the person she was then; you must see it as I do, Mrs. Betty! Mr. Maitland ought to act generously about it, and not to leave all the disagreeable part to Alice. It is a most awkward affair,' says she, 'and then that old Maitland is such a violent sort of person, he will be for prosecuting for breach of promise of marriage, or some such thing, and we shall have Mr. Henry and Sir Lynam fighting a duel; and these things, you know, would get into the newspapers, and that is such a thing! especially where a young girl is concerned. I must get Mrs. Twisleden to talk to him; he is a sensible person, and Mr. Maitland ought to be reasonable.' So talked Mrs. Franklin, as people talk who are too weak to do a wrong thing boldly.

"Sir Lynam was with Miss Franklin and her mother, when poor Mr. Maitland came first; he was with them the next day when he came again; the one staid against the other; hour after hour went on, callers came and went, and yet the two rivals staid.

"'Miss Franklin,' at length said poor Maitland, in a tone of determination, 'I shall return to London to-morrow, but before I go, I must have half-an-hour's conversation with you alone.'

"Sir Lynam looked eager, and seemed as if he would himself refuse this for her.

"'The evening is fine,' returned she, with an appearance of great equanimity, 'there is a full half-hour before I dress—will you walk with me, on the terrace?'

" The terrace, as you may remember, runs along
the front of the house, and as this took place in the
library, was exactly in face of the room. Sir Lynam
took his seat in one of the windows, which appeared
to me a very impertinent, not to say offensive
thing ;—whilst I, who, I am free to confess, was no
little interested, retired to my own room, where,
unseen, I might still get an occasional glimpse of
the two.

" They walked backward and forward, for some
time ; they were in deep discourse and spoke low,
although, it was evident, that it was not without
great warmth and excitement, on the part of Maitland. In turning, I once caught a glimpse of her
face ; it was flushed, and she looked both angry and
distressed. Whether she did not choose to be so
narrowly observed by Sir Lynam, or whether she
was now first aware that he was observing them, and
she thus chose to reprove him, I know not ; but after
having paced the terrace for some time, she turned
into a side walk, which led into the shrubbery, and
thus was lost to the view of the whole house.

" The bell rang for dressing ; the bell rang for
dinner ; half-an-hour passed, and then an hour ; and
but for the moon, which had risen in the meantime,
it must have been quite dark, and Alice was not yet
returned. Mrs. Franklin came up into my room,
quite alarmed. ' He is such a violent young man,'
said she, ' I am terrified beyond words ; there is no
knowing what a desperate man may do ! suppose, in
his madness, he should murder her !'

" ' She has done very wrong,' said I, for I had
been thinking over the affair, and I was brought up

to that pitch in which one speaks out the truth
unsparingly ; 'very wrong, indeed, has she done, if
she has cast off an old tried friend for a hypocrite,
like Sir Lynam. She will repent of it, one day or
another, as sure as she is alive !' said I, warmly.

" Mrs. Franklin made me no reply, but went out of
my room with the air of one very much insulted.

" The next moment, as I, myself, left my room, I
met Alice, coming up the great staircase,— she
walked slowly,—her thick veil was down over her
face, and she took not the slightest notice of me in
passing. She excused herself, on the plea of indisposition, from appearing at dinner, and Sir Lynam
took his leave.

" Everything that is done now-a-days at the hall is
soon a subject of village notoriety, and the interesting
fact of a handsome lover following the heiress from
London, and finding a rival in the person of Sir Lynam
Thicknisse, who is too well known here to be beloved,
created, as you may imagine, quite an excitement.

" The next day, Mrs. Joplin, the respectable landlady of the Thicknisse Arms, came up with a letter
which poor Maitland had intrusted to her care for
Miss Franklin ; and Perigord, who you may remember
is sister to Mrs. Joplin, and who, like everybody else,
is very angry at the encouragement given here to Sir
Lynam, brought her up into my room. The good
landlady's heart was brimful of sympathy for her
unhappy guest. My best way therefore will be, to
give you a detailed account of what happened after
Mr. Maitland left the hall, as much as may be in
her own words.

" ' He did not return,' said she, 'last night till

after eleven; he looked wretched and ill, and seemed like one perplexed and bewildered in a miserable dream; it made my heart ache to see him, and I determined to wait on him myself. He threw himself into a chair, and asked for pen, ink, and paper; but when he attempted to write he could not make a letter, his hand trembled so.'

"'I wish to be alone, my good landlady,' said he in a tone so mild, yet dejected, that Mrs. Joplin declares she could not help crying. 'Pardon me, Sir,' said she, determined not to seem as if she noticed his agitation, 'but I have got a nice little supper for you, a brace of partridges done to a turn, and an apple-tart with a touch of the quince in it. I have made them ready myself, and I 've some capital old port.'

"'What time is it?' asked he, taking out his watch, 'I forgot to wind up my watch last night,' said he. 'Half-past eleven, Sir,' said she, thinking to herself, 'poor dear gentleman, and no wonder he forgot to wind up his watch.'

"'I did not think it was so late,' said he, pushing aside the pen and paper, 'you may bring me in the supper.'

"Mrs. Joplin declares she never took such pains to set any meal out so temptingly as she did this, for it would have done her good to see him eat.

"'What time does the London coach go through to-morrow?' asked he. 'At ten o'clock,' she told him, and then informed him that supper was served.

"'I have all that is needful,' said he, glancing at the table. 'I thank you, my good landlady;—my bed-room, which is adjoining this, is ready I see;— I shall need nothing more.'

" ' It will be a pleasure to wait on you, Sir,' said she ; ' do allow me to stay, the smell of the supper won't be pleasant in the room after you're done.'

" ' I thank you, I thank you, my good landlady,' said he, ' but I wish to be alone—you will do me a favour by leaving me alone ! '

" ' I wished him good night, and went out without another word,' said Mrs. Joplin, ' for thinks I to myself, I know now I 'm a great bore to him ; anybody but him would have cursed and sworn in my face, and he 's as mild as an angel. Well, no sooner was I out than I heard him quietly bolt the door after me, but not with a great riot as if to let me know how glad he was I was gone, but as quietly as possible that I might not hear it. Now I call that,' said Mrs. Joplin, ' showing a very good heart !' I quite agreed in her opinion, and so will you.

" ' I went to bed,' continued she, ' but bless me, I could not close an eye ; my bed-room was next to that in which he sate, and the wall was but a thin one ; and there was he, poor gentleman, walking up and down all the livelong night, and all the while sighing as if his heart would break. I know how it is, said I to myself, yon young lady up at the hall has turned off this young gentleman for that creature Sir Lynam ! And would you believe it, Mrs. Betty,' said she, ' Sir Lynam himself slept in the best bed-room on the other side of me, and though that wall was of a regular thickness, I could hear him snoring away like a pig ! I only wished Miss Franklin could have been where I was. I could not help crying, said she, ' as I lay in bed ; but as towards morning all seemed quiet in his room I dropped asleep.

"'About nine o'clock,' continued she, 'his bell rang—I answered it myself, and, Lord love you, Mrs. Betty, he had not taken bit nor sup; the supper stood just as I had left it. Oh Lord!' exclaimed I, seeing this, 'I fear your honour did not relish your supper.' 'It was excellent,' said he, 'most excellent, but I was not well last night, I had no appetite for supper.' 'He never had his clothes off that night,' said Mrs. Joplin, 'nor had he touched the bed; and never,' said she, 'if I live to be a hundred years old, shall I forget his countenance.'

"'The coach goes at ten, you say,' said he; 'let me have a cup of coffee and some dry toast.' 'I cleared away the supper things,' said she, 'and set him out as pretty a little breakfast as I knew how; ham, and anchovy-essence, and everything I thought that give a relish. Mighty little, however, did he take; two cups of coffee, a few inches of dry toast, an egg, and that was all.'

"'And now my good landlady,' said he, when I had cleared all away, 'may I request one favour from you?' He was as pale as death while he spoke, and it seemed to me that it was all that ever he could do to keep calm. 'Lord! Sir,' said I, 'any manner of thing;' and I was every bit as near crying even as he. 'Will you then take charge of a letter—of this letter?' said he, taking it from his side-pocket; 'it must go to the hall immediately; I wish it to be delivered into Miss Franklin's hand.' 'I never,' said Mrs. Joplin, deeply affected as she spoke, 'shall forget how he spoke that name; he made a little pause before he could bring it out, and when he had said it—Lord! what an expression came over his face,

If he had been a woman he must have fainted; but as it was, he seemed to master himself.' 'And you'll do me a very great favour if you'll undertake this,' said he. 'I'll take it myself,' said I, and went out that I might not in any way intrude upon him.

" 'He paid like a prince,' said Mrs. Joplin, 'and I could not help saying to him as he was going, There is not a gentleman that I would more gladly see again than you, and I wish, if ever you come this way again, that you may be just as happy as you deserve! I don't believe, however,' continued she, 'that he heard or understood what I said, for he looked all the time like somebody lost; and I could not help saying to Willis the guard, who goes all the way to London, Just have an eye, Mr. Willis, to yon handsome young gentleman, and if you can show him any civility do, for he has some great trouble on his mind, and he pays like a prince. This last I put in because I know Willis, and though he is a good-hearted kind man, I know he thinks best of a passenger that pays well.

" 'Sir Lynam was leaning out of his room smoking a cigar as the coach drove off. I saw plain enough a malicious pleasure in his eye; but the poor London gentleman did not see him, and so I did not mind.'

" So far, my dear Elizabeth, Mrs. Joplin, and you, must pardon all this detail; it interested me, and I know it will interest you likewise, who know this unfortunate young gentleman better than I do.

" *Nov.* 21. This morning Miss Franklin and her mother drove out in the coach; she was veiled as she went from the house to the carriage, nor has she seen Sir Lynam to-day. To-morrow she and her mother dine with a small party at General Byerly's, with whose family a considerable intimacy exists.

"*Nov.* 22. Sir Lynam's groom is again at the gate with his master's horse; he has it appears been admitted to see her.

"I write no more at this moment, for the sufficient reason that my paper is quite full.

"Yours, as ever,

"BETTY THICKNISSE."

CHAPTER VII.

A BEAUTIFUL SPIRIT, AND TEA WITH A FRIEND.

IT was the end of November, cold dispiriting November. The rich and well-clothed, and amply provided for, sitting in warm rooms, without a worldly care to disturb them, could not resist its influence; it weighed down the heart of the anxious, and sent a feeling akin to despair into the bosom that wanted hope, and while it chilled to the bone made many a poor householder sigh over the price of fuel.

Philip Durant, who had gone on the Western Circuit with the Judges, had not yet returned, although shortly expected, and his young wife sate in their small room with her child. Her child was sleeping, and her thoughts were with her husband.

There was a knock at the door; the postman brought her a letter. Ah! a letter from her husband! Her eyes beamed, her cheek flushed, and, by the trembling anxiety with which she broke the seal, had any one been present they might have seen how dear the writer was to her. "Dear Philip," sighed she as she closed the letter, and with a tearful eye, whilst with all the humility of true love a prayer filled her heart, that God would make her worthy of his love.

The letter, however, was not a cheerful one,—the circuit had been very unproductive to the young barrister, and his father's strange and foolish marriage, which the papers had bruited far and wide, occasioned him many a mortification.

"I am glad," thought she, "that I parted with our expensive servant. I will manage with this little girl whilst he is away, and when he returns perhaps also we may; but at all events, I will be more prudent and careful than ever. Thank God for my husband! I will get his chambers nicely furnished for him—as nicely at least as my little means will allow; thank Heaven, I am not much known in London; my economy will neither humiliate me, nor be injurious to him."

With these thoughts in her heart, she seated herself at her writing-desk, took out a quantity of most neatly copied manuscript, which after turning over and looking through, and making here and there a word more legible, and then reading page after page, in another part, with deep interest, she in the end laid carefully together, and then tied up in a neat packet.

"Please God!" ejaculated she to herself, "that this may be successful. What a blessing it will be to us!"

She then took out a silk purse, from which she counted five guineas, which in fact were its contents. No miser ever looked at his secret hoard with more intense pleasure than did poor Gertrude at these five golden guineas; there was a light in her eye, and a crimson on her lovely cheek, which made her really beautiful.

"Thank God!" she again ejaculated, and was turning over in her mind the purpose to which this money was destined, when the child woke, and thoughts of her husband, which had till now filled her heart, gave place to thoughts of her ch.ld.

An hour after this time, we may see Gertrude, with her little maid-servant and child, on their way to Elizabeth Durant's; and somewhat later, we will look in and see the two sitting together in Elizabeth's chamber, in earnest and confidential discourse.

"I don't know," said Gertrude, "why I should have any objection to his knowing about it; but I would not for the world that he should know if I am unsuccessful. He has anxieties enough of his own, without my adding to them."

Elizabeth had a magazine in her hand, which Gertrude had brought her, and out of which she had been reading.

"But how exquisitely beautiful it is!" said she, closing the number; "so full of a fresh and joyous spirit, yet showing, at the same time, such knowledge of human nature. If you write like this, I wonder you did not long ago make your talent known to Philip."

Gertrude blushed. "I know not how it is exactly," said she, "but I am always so jealous of his esteem, I fancy he himself could write much better than I do, if he chose to try."

"Philip is a most accomplished and intellectual man,

dear Gertrude," said Elizabeth, smiling; "but without any disrespect to him, I question if he could write poetry like this, though he would feel it as deeply as any of us."

The two friends talked together of many things, and at length began to speak of Gertrude's life before she became acquainted with her husband.

" Ah!" said Gertrude, with a tear in her eye, and yet smiling, " I cannot help having a sort of compassion on myself when I look back to those dark, friendless years before I knew Philip. You know not, Elizabeth, how joyless my life was then; I had no one to sympathise with me; my feelings, my desires, my sufferings, were all locked in my own heart.

" As a child, I had been diffident and retiring; and when at twelve I lost my mother,—and oh how the knowledge of this must have embittered her death,— I was thrown among strangers. My guardian and his wife were a good kind of people; but he was a man in trade, who had made much money by a life of plodding and economy; he was a rigidly upright man, not so much from native elevation and integrity of character, as because honesty was, as he said times without end, the best policy. All kind of philosophy and poetry was to him a species of heresy; he was a Realist in the truest sense of the word; and knowing as he did so well how unpromising were my prospects in life, for my father, alas! had always been a speculator, and the little property he left was invested in companies and speculations—shares here and shares there—all which in the end proved mere bubbles, burst, and left me nothing. My guardian, therefore, was most anxious to prevent my having my father's failing, and scarcely ever did he open his lips to me without its being for the utterance of some prudential maxim. I was taught—but alas! I never learned—to repress my imagination, and everything approaching to sentiment in me was endeavoured to be crushed; and thus I, who was naturally imaginative, and full of feeling, learned betimes the dangerous art of concealment, and locking up all these beloved sins in my own breast, indulged them in secret only the more.

"My guardian died in my fifteenth year; and his wife, who had all her husband's prudence, without his generosity, informed me that the legacy of three hundred pounds which my guardian had left me, and which was my sole property, must be devoted to preparing and enabling me to gain my own livelihood, in a school. I had no will in the case; my former home was less attractive than ever, when my guardian, whom I now came to see had been my best friend, was gone, and any change I hoped would be for the better. I was placed as half-boarder for three years at a large establishment, where I was to perfect myself in every possible accomplishment, and to learn almost every modern tongue, after which I was to be received in the school as teacher, at a stated salary, or to have another situation equally good, found for me. My three years at Brussels were anything but sunshiny—still I made progress in all my studies. Music was my greatest delight, and I was considered so great a proficient, that as a sort of show-off person I was no little esteemed in the establishment. Of French, Italian, and German, I was considered perfect

mistress; and my oil-paintings were thought good
enough to be framed for the school drawing-room. I
was then eighteen, and I was beginning to look
forward to being independent.

"But oh, Elizabeth!" said she, after a moment-
ary pause, in which the recollection of that time had
rushed over her mind, "you know not what a life
is her's who is educating to be a teacher in a school!
She must be so mechanical, she must be so wise,
she must be so prudent and exemplary: there is so
little forbearance shown to her, so little allowance
made for her! And if she should have weak health,
as I had, and suffer physically from cold and over-
exertion, and morally from want of sympathy; if
she should lie awake half the night, and then fall
asleep just before it is time to get up, God have mercy
on her! And then that depression of spirit, and that
deep longing, which eats into the very soul, for all
the little charities of life, for kind words, and fellowship, and love! Yes, Elizabeth, few girls of eighteen
were as highly accomplished as I was—but may
Heaven forbid that many young hearts of eighteen
should have had likewise the same experience in
hardship and sorrow.

"Many a time," continued she, "have I envied
the commonest maid-servant; who, when her work
was done, could sit down of an evening and complain to her fellows of her place, and grumble about
her grievances, and give warning, and take another
service at the end of her quarter. It was not so with
me; I had no exact equal in the school—I was a
half-boarder—looked down upon both by teachers
and scholars; I was apprenticed to the establish-

ment, and to leave it, nay even to complain, was to ruin my own poor prospects. It was dark enough, truly; but still it was not wholly without light. I had pleasure in my own progress, a turn for languages and an unquestionable talent for music, and some little likewise for painting. Notwithstanding all this, however, my natural reserve and my doubt of myself grew more and more. I never sate down to the instrument before any one without trembling. I opened my heart to no one, but I indulged more and more in those day-dreams and reveries to which I had always been addicted. At length, however, my reveries found words, and I began to essay little poems—but oh! I should as soon have thought of crying aloud in a market-place, as of showing my little effusions to any one; all remained locked in my own breast.

" About the time my term was completed a lady of Brighton having written in quest of an assistant in her school, with the most flattering promises of partnership, and I know not what besides, the situation was offered to me. It promised well; and I, full of the most buoyant hope, and with I know not what patriotism burning in my heart, set my foot again on my native soil, my own mistress, as I hoped, and with a prosperous life before me. Alas! it was not many days before I looked back to the abundant table and well-to-do establishment at Brussels, as to a sort of Paradise from which I was banished. The poor lady here was just on the verge of bankruptcy.—Good heaven! what a fearful time was that four months!—a miserably cold winter, and every means of life and warmth inadequately supplied, with a wretched outside show of profusion.

"My health would not stand it—the physician whom I was obliged to consult ordered my immediate return home, a generous diet, and repose. 'Return home!' repeated I to myself, 'and where in this world have I a home?' for the widow of my guardian had in the course of the last three years married a second husband, with a grown family of sons and daughters. Necessity, however, has no law, and as my life depended on some change, I wrote to her; told her my exact state, and solicited not only her advice, but if possible, that I might be permitted to spend a few months with her, for after all my experience of life my heart warmed to her as to a mother.

"She was by no means a bad-hearted woman, and, considerably touched by my letter, she obtained from her husband and his family an invitation for me to visit them. My aunt's step-sons and daughters were handsome, dashing, expensive young people, who lived for show and the enjoyment of life, and as was natural, perhaps, not only looked down on me— as on the poor teacher in a school, but made me feel too that they did so. Theirs, however, was a house of plenty; and eating and drinking of the very best were grudged to none. There, too, I had repose, and that was better for me even than more generous food: it was fine summer weather too; there were extensive gardens and grounds, and to me, solitary as I still was, it was like a heavenly life. After I had been two months in the family, and was beginning to have uncomfortable feelings if I saw anybody glancing on that part of the Times newspaper which contained

advertisements for governesses, Philip came on a
visit to the sons of the family; they and he had been
college friends, although very different characters all
of them; one of those friendships it was which exists
in youth, but must of necessity die in manhood.
He came," said Gertrude, her cheek flushing while
she spoke, "came for a visit of two weeks. How
strange—how incredible was it to me, that he, clever,
manly, the son of the great lawyer, Sir Thomas
Durant—himself, as I was told, a young lawyer of
great promise,—the scholar, the gentleman,—oh,
how strange was it when the consciousness first came
to me that he loved me, and not only that he loved
me, but that he offered me his hand! Elizabeth,
I never shall forget that time;—I loved him all the
while so intensely, as I believed so hopelessly; he
was my first, my only love; I looked up to him as
to one so infinitely above me, it would have seemed
presumption in me to have raised my thoughts to
him, other than as a sort of divinity.

" He and the family he was visiting had very little
in common; he very rarely went out with the sons
on their shooting excursions, and seldom played bil-
liards with them. The daughters dressed splendidly,
and received and paid visits. I was a quiet little insignificant person, for whom nobody cared, and of
whom nobody thought. Philip stopped at home and
read to me while I mended my clothes. I supposed
he might fall in love with one of my aunt's step-
daughters; they sang and played to him of an evening: I remember, one evening, his saying to me, ' Do
you not play, Gertrude?' I was so thrilled by his
calling me *Gertrude*: but I thought instantly, I am

only like a child or servant to him—and I was humiliated. I replied, ' Yes.' ' Why then do you not? I wish you would,' said he. Nobody seconded his wish, but he was resolute, and led me to the instrument himself. I was always timid in playing before any one; then I knew, too, that this grand two-hundred guinea instrument was the idol of the house: they were jealous of the keys being touched; everybody was silent in the room, and I must play, not only before them, but before Philip. I played Beethoven's Adelaide: it was a favourite piece of mine; and though I would have given worlds to have played it well, I never before succeeded so little to my own satisfaction. ' And do you sing?' asked Philip, coming forward towards me as I ran from the instrument. ' Yes, a little,' said I, almost ready to cry, for I was nervous and terrified; 'but to-night I cannot.' I never shall forget the expression of Philip's eye—it seemed to me filled with unspeakable affection; but I dared not at the moment believe so, and, unable any longer to stay in the room, I went to my own chamber and wept.

" He and I were often left alone together, for the family thought so little of me, that they never could imagine me a rival. He sate with me all one morning, and read Campbell's Pleasures of Hope. The poem was well known to me, but till that morning it seemed as if I had never thoroughly understood it, or appreciated its beauties; and again I wept, I hardly knew why—nor did I dare to look up, lest he should see my tears. He laid down the book, and asked me to walk with him; it seemed to me such a condescension in him, and I dressed myself as nicely as I could, because I felt so pleased. How infinitely

happy I was, as he asked me to take his arm when
we left the house, and then I remember I thought
how dreadful it would be when he was gone; and
then how I should live for years and years on the
remembrance of him. 'I shall never marry,' thought
I to myself, ' for, after knowing Philip, how can I
love anybody else ?'

"On that morning, Elizabeth, he asked me to be
his wife! I could hardly believe my senses; I
thought it must be a dream;—yet no! there he was
before me, so kind, so earnest, so sincere; I could not
doubt it, but someway or other I felt as if it were
too good to last! I thought—oh, I know not what I
thought!

"When the family knew that I, the poor, despised
Cinderella of the household, had won the heart of
the great lawyer's son, my position there became a
very unpleasant one. I had evidently interfered
with family arrangements, which, under any circumstances, could not fail of displeasing, but in this instance made mine almost an unpardonable sin.

"Philip told me exactly what was his position at
home and with his father, and I did not expect to
marry for years I advertised for a situation in a
school, and took the first which offered. I was now
so unspeakably happy in myself, that everything
wore a new and different aspect. I found my new
situation by no means an unpleasant one; a light heart
makes all duties and labours light, even the most
unvarying and harassing. For years I could have
been happy in this situation, had not my health again
given way. What was I to do? I concealed my
illness till I could conceal it no longer, and Mrs

Lewis, the lady of the establishment, insisted then on my writing to my aunt. Her reply only increased my difficulty: it was kind, but she could, she said, give me no invitation to her house; she hinted of her own private troubles, inclosed me five pounds, and bade me not look to her again for assistance. I rallied as much as I could, and thought when spring came I should be better. I determined if possible to keep all from Philip's knowledge; but, suspecting something was amiss, from my letters, he himself came down. When he saw me and heard the physician's opinion, he would hear of nothing but our marriage; he himself, he said, would take care of me and provide for me. He was so hopeful, so determined, so kind, that I could not refuse. But oh! Elizabeth, how ashamed was I to think of my poverty; physicians' fees had consumed more than my half-year's salary, and I had very little money to buy wedding-clothes with—a woman feels these things. I was married in a white muslin dress, which cost but eight shillings, and which I made myself; I had my straw bonnet, which was in its second year, cleaned for the occasion, and I trimmed it with book-muslin, because that was less costly than ribbon. I could not help crying as I did this, for I seemed such a poor bride; and, could I have dressed myself in the most costly bridal apparel, I should not have thought it too much for the occasion.

"Never, however, was a bride so happy and so proud as I was. Philip seemed so too. We made no bridal excursion, for the simple reason that we could not afford it; and we came at once to our quiet, unexpensive lodgings, where we mutually agreed to live as economically as possible, in the belief that more prosperous days would come, and in the meantime Philip hoped to be reconciled with his father.

"Happy, however, as we were, prosperous days came not, and Sir Thomas was as implacable as ever, and I, loving my husband as I did, could not help being distressed by the anxious expression of his countenance, which I knew he endeavoured to conceal from me.

"He knew nothing of my little attempts at authorship, for I thought humbly of them myself; and I knew his taste in literature to be so good that I feared lowering myself in his estimation by my poor attempts, particularly as I had heard him more than once express disapprobation of women thrusting themselves into notoriety; he thought it unfeminine. When, however, I was obliged to make so many demands on his purse, in expectation of our little one's birth, I took a desperate resolution one day, and copying out a few poems took them to the editor of this magazine. I took them to him because I had heard Mrs. Lewis speak of him; he was her brother, and she always spoke of him with pride, as a kind-hearted and honourable man. He desired me to leave them with him and to call again. I did so; and to my great surprise he offered me two guineas for them. How thankful I was! more especially as he expressed a desire to see something more from my pen. I paid him a second visit, and on that occasion received from him five guineas. He was extremely kind. He is an elderly gentleman, and that set me more at my ease with him; he appeared, too, to take the most lively interest in me. Although I never avowed my name, he asked me of my acquirements— if I had ever attempted translation, or had ever tried my hand at prose. Prose, he said, sold much better than poetry, and that he would like to see whatever I did in this way; and much more that was most encouraging. Of all this I have said nothing to Philip, for I was afraid that he might think much less favourably of my productions than even Mr. ——, and I could not bear that he should despise me. I thought still that I would wait and see if my prose were successful; and then, if it were so, he should know all."

"And your prose," said Elizabeth, "have you yet offered that to Mr. —— ?"

" It is here," said Gertrude, taking up the packet of manuscript. "It will make two volumes. It is a simple tale, drawn from my own experience, and carried on into the future—into such a future as I would covet for myself and Philip. It is a tale of virtue, not of vice, in which I have endeavoured to make goodness and virtue interesting for their own intrinsic beauty and interest; which, after all, really need no contrast of vice to make them attractive. If this work be successful," repeated Gertrude, "I will then show it to Philip, for it is the best thing I have done. I have written it since I have been married—since I have understood things better, and since I have gained a juster appreciation of life and human nature. Before I knew Philip I took such one-sided views of life—all was so dark to me then! I had so little reliance on goodness and affection— in fact, till I knew him, I knew nothing that was true and excellent."

Mrs. Durant was in most happy humour to-day, and received even the wife and child of Philip Durant with kindness; nor was she in the least annoyed that, while Elizabeth and the young mother had such a long private conference together, the little nursemaid and child were left to keep her company. The true cause of all this was, that the long-talked-of letter had been, this very day, received from Alice Franklin.

Alice knew nothing of the contents of Mrs. Betty's letters, and she gave her own colouring, of course, to affairs. The spirit of the letter seemed kindness and candour itself, and Mrs. Durant was charmed with it. Alice disclaimed the idea of a petty annuity of fifty pounds a year; she begged Mrs. Durant to draw that sum at once, from her banker's, and promised unbounded liberality for the future. She hoped, she said, that Elizabeth, in the early spring, would pay her a long visit. Mrs. Betty had shown her the room which Elizabeth had used during her former visit there, and she should consider, she said, that chamber as sacred to her friend; before she came, however, she would have it re-furnished for her; she had fixed in her own mind on the style of furnishing, she said; and she was sure her friend would like it, and then that room should always be called Elizabeth Durant's room.

Mrs. Betty, she said, would still continue to reside at Starkey—at least she wished her to do so,—but the old lady was, she said, it must be confessed, a very peculiar person, very uncompromising and very free-spoken; she and her mother had already had several little differences with her, but, for her part,

she could make great allowances for her; she had
always had her own way, (that was a great mistake
of Miss Franklin's, and so Elizabeth knew), and,
continued the letter, she belonged to the old school,
and those old-fashioned people were always so
difficult to manage. Of Sir Lynam Thicknisse,
Alice said not one word; of Henry Maitland, she
wrote thus :—" Of course you have heard about poor
Maitland ; it is all at an end between us now. I
wish he had not come at present ; he was to wait for
my permission, but he always is so impetuous ;
things might have been very different had he only
waited awhile. Still I do not blame him, and I
know that he has suffered deeply. A little hasty, I
myself may have been, but then he hurried me into
it ; he himself hurried things to this conclusion.
It has been, altogether, an unfortunate affair ; and,
now it is over, I wish him, from the bottom of my
soul, some one more worthy of his good and amiable
qualities than I ever have been."

Elizabeth sighed and shook her head over this
letter ; whilst Mrs. Durant, in the humour she then
was, could see nothing at all blameable in Alice's
conduct. Her promised liberality smoothed over all
faults, and made Mrs. Durant not only satisfied with
her, but, just then, with all the world.

" And now, where are you going ?" asked she,
as she saw her daughter dressed, ready to go out
with Gertrude.

" We are going," replied Gertrude, cheerfully,
" to make five pounds, if possible, do the work of
ten. I want to make Philip's chambers more comfortable and more respectable-looking, before his

K

return. I want a carpet, table, window-curtains,— a world of things out of my five pounds; and, as two heads are better than one, in difficult affairs, I have enlisted Elizabeth as my assistant."

" And what parcel have you got there, Elizabeth ?" asked the mother, who was in a talkative humour, glancing on the packet of manuscripts, which her daughter had in her hand.

" It is Gertrude's," replied Elizabeth.

" And shall you go anywhere near Glynn's bank ? it is in Lombard Street, you know," asked her mother.

Elizabeth thought they would.

" Then call," said Mrs. Durant, " and present that order : we may just as well have the money as let it lie in the bank—we shall get no interest for it there."

Elizabeth tore the order from Alice's letter, and said she would do as her mother wished.

" I shall leave my little one as a pledge for your daughter," said Gertrude, as they were just going out.

" That's quite right," said Mrs. Durant. " But stop a moment—you shall have tea with us when you return; bring some muffins with you, Elizabeth, and I'll have the tea-table ready and water boiling against you return—you'll be cold enough, and a cup of tea will be comfortable. You must take a cab home, Mrs. Philip, and you may just as well take it at eight o'clock as at six."

Nothing requires more deliberation, nothing requires so much pains-taking, as the making five pounds go as far as ten. For instance, a second-hand carpet—and the fair wife of the young barrister did

not aspire to a new one—a second-hand carpet, we
say, as good as the one for which fifty shillings is
here demanded, might, in another place, perhaps, be
obtained for thirty shillings; but then, that other
place, perhaps, may be two miles off; well, that
does not matter—the two miles must be gone over,—
and, as people who have the important affair in hand
of buying, honestly and honourably, ten pounds'
worth of things with only five pounds, cannot be supposed to have much money to spend in coach-fare,
they must walk every foot of the way, even if it be
in dismal November.

It was a very arduous undertaking this, but
nothing daunted, the two young friends determined
to accomplish it, if not to-day, at least to-morrow.
The five guineas were still in Gertrude's purse; the
manuscript had been left at the publisher's; the fifty
pounds had been received from Glynn's bank, and
then it was getting too late to do anything more: so
counting the difference between new window-curtains
of cheap moreen, and second-hand ones of damask,
and contriving how the carpet of thirty shillings
might be cut to the size of the room, every bad
piece cut out, joined again in the pattern, which
they blessed themselves was a very good one to join,
and made to look as good as new,—to say nothing
of the bed-side carpet, which might be pieced
together of what remained, they found quite enough
to occupy them on their way home. It is by no
means impossible, we can assure our readers, for a
question of economy and contrivance to become quite
fascinating; it was so on the present occasion: the
two grew enthusiastic, and Elizabeth declared she

would go again with her friend on the morrow, and
then help her to fit all down and make all complete ;
and so they reached home by gas-light, never thinking
—not they—of the muffins they had promised to
bring with them.

Well, it did not matter ! they did not need
muffins, in the temper they two were, to make tea
both welcome and agreeable; toast would do every
bit as well—nay, even bread and butter.   Mrs.
Durant, however, was a little put out of humour
about the muffins, she had set her mind on them ; nor
was it till she had counted over her fifty pounds
three or four times, and drank a cup of the good,
hot tea, which Elizabeth made, and eaten a couple
of the pieces of the nice toast, which Gertrude
herself had toasted, that she returned to her former
good humour, and then she began to tell how good
the child had been,—how long he had slept,—how
he had taken half a tea-cup full of milk and water :
and thus they all together seemed the best friends on
the face of the earth.

Just before tea was ended, Mr. Netley came in.
Poor old gentleman ! ever since his niece and her
daughter had left him, he had seemed like an uneasy
spirit that could find rest nowhere.   In his own
mind he was very little satisfied with Alice's good
fortune ; it had made him, and the property he had
to leave, of very little consequence, and besides this
it had removed them from him.   He came very
often to the Durants', and Mrs. Durant was beginning to think that it would not be at all amiss if he
would substitute herself and her daughter in his
house at Richmond, in the place of the Franklins ;

she would have suggested the thing herself, but then she thought it had much better come from him; and as it really was so self-evident, no doubt before long it would. Such an idea, however, never came into the old gentleman's head. He was dissatisfied with what he heard of Alice's mode of conducting herself at Starkey, and it did him good to come to the Durants' and grumble, that was all.

With Philip Durant's marriage, Mr. Netley was already acquainted; he had seen his wife and liked her, so when he came in this evening, all met as friends. He, too, had received a letter from Alice, and he came with it now in his pocket.

"She writes mighty cool about everything," said he, "and seems never to think that anything she can do is wrong. She talks of 'I shall do this, and I shall do that,' just as if she had been mistress of Starkey all her days. She says it is all at an end between her and Maitland, just with as much indifference as she might say, 'My old blue silk gown is done for!' I have not patience with such coolness; she says she supposes I shall hear all from Maitland, but she had her reasons for what she did. To be sure! the man who was hanged at the Old Bailey, last week, had his reasons for murdering his wife! I would not give a fig for reasons that are good for nothing; why Maitland, poor fellow, is ill of a brain fever, and whether he'll live or die there s no knowing. She had her reasons, I dare say!

"Old Maitland threatens hard," continued he, "what he'll do. She'll bring a pretty house over her head—that's my notion! And then there's this Sir Lynam Thicknisse;—old Maitland sen* me a

Durham paper this morning, in which are queer hints about her marrying him! It is not decent, all this; and the old lady hardly been dead these two months, and he, the profligate that he is! why, it was he that set the bells ringing for the old lady's death! The girl's a fool!" said he, " her head is turned with her prosperity! She wants me to go and see her; says a great deal about it, and I must do her the justice to say, that she writes very prettily and very affectionately; she says that she has set aside a couple of rooms for me;—wants me to take Jonathan with me. I know how it is, she wants to palm me off as her rich old London uncle! and so I must not go without my man-servant; but though she is the lady of Starkey she can't make me any but plain Nehemiah Netley, who for the better part of his days was a haberdasher on Ludgate Hill, and who began the world with eighteenpence, and that I'll say before any lord or lady in the land! However, I mean," said he, " to take her at her word and go and pay her a visit, though it is winter. If I like what I see, why I'll stay,—if not, I'll e'en come back again. I shall start to-morrow morning, so whatever you have to send I must have to-night'"

There was no time for writing. Mr. Netley was intrusted, therefore, with verbal messages from both Elizabeth and her mother. Mrs. Durant said she meant to write soon herself, though she had given up writing letters. Elizabeth said she meant to write, and to Mrs. Betty too; and, after promises on his part to deliver all faithfully, he volunteered to take Gertrude, her little maid and child home, in the coach which was to convey him to Richmond.

CHAPTER VIII.

A CLOUD BY THE FIRESIDE; AND WHAT SHALL BE DONE NOW?

ALICE had given to herself great satisfaction by allowing Mrs. Durant to receive fifty pounds from her banker's ; so much so, indeed, that she wished she had made it a hundred at once. She was pleased too that she had pressed her uncle to come, for though she did not exactly wish him to accept the invitation in the present state of affairs, and while his mind would be irritated about young Maitland, it was quite as well to show all customary respect to him. She felt certain in her own mind that he would not undertake the journey during the winter ; he would, most likely, wait till spring, till long days and warm ones came, for she knew perfectly his aversion to cold weather and long journeys.

" Poor old gentleman !" That very hour, whilst she was thinking this, a week or more perhaps after she had written her letter, he too was thinking his thoughts.

" Dear child !" mused he to himself, " I am glad she remembers her old uncle ! and with all her faults I am very fond of her ! She has, it is true, behaved shamefully to poor Maitland ;— but I dare say I can set all right again,— her mother ought to have seen after this, but women. . . . " Mr. Netley, it must be remembered, was an old bachelor : " Women," mused he, " from the very creation of the world were always taking some wrong step or another ; they are not fit to be trusted, poor things ; so I'll e'en go and see if I can't set things straight between her and Maitland !"

So thought the good old gentleman, and made preparations for the journey. He ordered Jonathan, his servant, to hold himself in readiness to accompany him ; which was no small delight to the ancient domestic, for thus he should be able to satisfy every body, baker, butcher, grocer, and even the family washerwoman, as to the exact degree of grandeur to which Miss Alice was advanced.

Mr. Netley did not set off quite so early as he expected however, for when all was ready for the journey, and the next day was fixed upon for setting out, he took it into his head to order a new suit of clothes for his servant: and thus a delay of ten days ensued, during which some circumstances occurred at Starkey, by no means unworthy of record.

Whatever might be Alice's real feelings after reading the letter which Mrs. Joplin, of the Thicknisse Arms, delivered into her hands, nobody ever knew them ; still it is a fact, that she was scarcely seen by any one for several days; and the persons who composed the small dinner-party at General Byerly's, and who were invited to meet the heiress and her mother, found fertile subject for conjecture and gossip in her pale dejected countenance, and in the rumour, which spread far and wide, of a heart-broken rejected London lover. Sir Lynam Thicknisse too, not only observed her altered appearance, but must have had some little apprehension for himself, from the step he took immediately after the call which he made upon her, and which was chronicled in Mrs. Betty's last letter.

"Good bye, Miss Franklin," said he at parting; "I give you seven days to recover your spirits in. In that time I shall again have the pleasure of seeing you as beautiful, and I hope, as gay as ever. I go this evening to Durham on important business."

There was something Alice thought presumptuous in Sir Lynam's manner, something too, offensive in his words; and she who, without the slightest intention of returning favour to Maitland, had already drawn comparisons between the two to the disadvantage of Sir Lynam, bade him adieu with studied haughtiness and coldness.

To Durham Sir Lynam went, and sate down the next morning in the office of a lawyer named Metcalf. Metcalf and he were old acquaintance, and this was not the first time that they two had met on the particular business which had now brought them together.

"It is an excellent thing," said Sir Lynam, "and one which properly managed may give me great power over her; I'll double your fees, Metcalf, if this be accomplished to my wishes."

"That she has no present right to Starkey," said the lawyer, "no right at all during the natural life of Mrs. Betty Thicknisse, is as clear as daylight, as you may see in the codicil to Sir Timothy's will, of which this is a copy." And although Sir Lynam knew the codicil almost by heart, Metcalf read it again: "And furthermore I, the said Sir Timothy Thicknisse, demise that the estate and property of Starkey shall be held by the direct heirs, so long as any of them, male or female, remain in the third descent; and after the death of the last only to revert to the then existing descendant or descendants, male or female, of the said Joan Merivale, as before stated." "Thus you see, Sir Lynam," said the lawyer, "it is as I imagined; this reversion, on the death of the late Sir Sampson, passed legally to his sister, Mrs. Betty Thicknisse, and only on her death can revert to Miss Franklin."

"I see that," said Sir Lynam; "I want to establish no right of claim for Mrs. Betty—I want not to dispossess Miss Franklin, but merely—"

"Oh, I understand you perfectly," said Metcalf; "you make use of this knowledge as you best know how."

"No codicil has ever been acknowledged at Starkey," said Sir Lynam, not deeming it necessary to notice his friend's remark further—"the late Lady Thicknisse knew nothing of it—nor Mr. Twisleden—what think you?"

"I think," said Metcalf, "that the late Lady Thicknisse was lawyer good enough to know that such a codicil made her possession of Starkey not worth an hour's purchase, and that it was probably destroyed; Mrs. Betty has always been looked upon as a sort of—" Metcalf paused, tapped his forehead, and looked as if he meant the action to express a great deal.

"I understand you," said Sir Lynam: "not quite so sharp as some people. It would be quite throwing the place away to let it get into her hands."

Metcalf said he quite agreed with him it would, and that if Sir Lynam played his cards well, he might turn the knowledge he had thus obtained to

great account with the heiress, but that some decided step must be taken immediately, for that other
lawyers might think of examining the probate copy
of the will, and then Mrs. Betty would commence a
suit and carry it, for that not all the lawyers in
England could decide it against her : she might live
twenty years, and all that while Miss Franklin could
not claim a sixpence.

Sir Lynam thought that in twenty years Alice
would be no longer young, and twenty years of un-
thrift would leave him a beggar ; besides which, he
had of late counted so confidently on carrying off so
triumphantly both Starkey and the heiress, it would
never do to lose it, for if it got into Mrs. Betty's
hands, he should never think of marrying her, nor
indeed, with all his art, should he ever have any
chance of succeeding, were he to try.

" To be sure," he said, " something must be done
immediately." Metcalf must devise some plan for
cutting off Mrs. Betty's claim.

The lawyer sate and thought, and so did Sir
Lynam, and the more he thought the better he was
pleased. This discovery would give him power over
Alice, and if she consented to disinherit Mrs. Betty,
it must be done with his knowledge; she might be
cold or haughty as she then would, but she would
have committed herself with him—he should have
a secret of hers in his keeping, and that was so much
power gained over her. For one moment the question suggested itself—had she not high-flown romantic
notions of honour and generosity? which would make
her scorn a base action—might she not, for the sake
of the éclat of the thing, throw herself on the mercy

of Mrs. Betty, and make terms with her? That would ruin all; for that would ally the two, make the two fast friends, make Alice dependent on Mrs. Betty, and she, he well knew, was no friend of his. All this *might* be, and if it were probable, it were alarming; but a few moments' consideration dismissed Sir Lynam's fear: Alice was too much flattered by the entire possession of Starkey to share it with any one; he felt pretty sure that she would hold it fast now she had got it. Metcalf thought the same; and though Sir Lynam did not open out all his views to his lawyer, he found no little satisfaction in his lawyer volunteering an opinion on this subject which was so perfectly according to his wishes. Next, some little difficulty occurred about Mr. Twisleden; the old gentleman was a most respectable man, and could boast of a character without a blemish—what part would he take in the affair? Neither one or the other could say positively; Sir Lynam, however, thought from his own private observation, but he did not tell Metcalf so, that Twisleden would do exactly what Alice wished. He must be made acquainted, however, with this unlooked for discovery; Metcalf, it was decided, should write to him, should desire an immediate interview either at Starkey or in Durham, and Sir Lynam should wait in Durham for the result.

Whilst all this was going on at twenty miles' distance, domestic disunion seemed to have settled down at Starkey. Mrs. Betty's sympathies had been so much excited by the little narrative of the hostess of the Thicknisse Arms respecting Maitland, that the kind-hearted old lady could not get him out of her mind; she thought of him and shed tears, and as she wept she only grew more angry and out of patience with Alice. Sir Lynam came and went just as usual; and without knowing that Alice and he had parted coldly, she censured her with a severity almost unnatural to a being so gentle as Mrs. Betty.

"I declare I must speak out my mind," at last she said to herself; "it is only right I should; she is a lovely young creature, with all her faults; she is tempted beyond her strength by this great inheritance; she comes here a stranger, in ignorance of people's characters; and her mother wants sense, or discernment, or something, not to see through a designing wretch like Sir Lynam."

Warmed by the generous desire of saving Alice from a false step, Mrs. Betty took her netting in her hand, and went to take coffee with Alice and her mother that same evening. She had not done so of late, and the two were filled with surprise when she entered. Unfortunately, there had just been a slight misunderstanding between them respecting Mr. Netley's visit, and neither of them were in the happiest of tempers. Alice lay on the sofa reading a new novel, which was just then published, and Mrs. Franklin was writing.

Both mother and daughter looked up at Mrs. Betty's entrance; both wondered what had made her come; and then, after an exchange of the merest commonplaces of the day, both pursued their occupations as before. Mrs. Betty thought that presently they would put them aside out of respect to her, but Mrs. Betty was not of importance enough for that. One hour went on; the mother still wrote, and the daughter still read ; and had the poor old lady had the temper of an angel, she could not have helped being chagrined.

The servant brought in coffee ; Alice bade him make it and hand it round : she was too much absorbed by her book to leave it. Mrs. Franklin drank her coffee, chatted a very little with Mrs. Betty, and then apologised by continuing her writing. "She was writing," she said, "to Mr. Netley, and must finish her letter that night." Alice read on, and Mrs. Betty tried, but in vain, to be in good humour. She might have returned to her own room, out she had always a great dislike to looking, as she called it, "huffy," so she sat where she was.

Presently Mr Twisleden came. Alice laid down her book and began to look lively. The old gentleman apologised for his visit, which, he said, was one of ousiness : he was now prepared, he said, to pay all the legacies. Alice declared that she never attended to business after dinner ; she began to talk of the book she had been reading, told him she had found an air to the song he had expressed a wish to hear her sing, and, so saying, sat down to her harp.

"The coquet ! the cold-hearted coquet !" thought Mrs. Betty, as she heard Alice's exquisite voice quaver forth its thrilling tones, and the poor old gentleman gazing on her with undisguised admiration.

Mrs. Franklin put aside her unfinished letter, and suggested yet another and yet another song for " dear old Mr. Twisleden." .

Which was the most foolish—mother or daughter —Mrs. Betty could not tell ; the fact was, Mrs. Franklin was so well pleased to see Alice again in good humour, that it made her quite lively, and all the more so, because she wished her daughter to feel that all was again smooth between them.

Mr. Twisleden sat and sat; Alice left her harp, and made the old gentleman sit down beside her, and guess charades; they grew so amazingly lively that it was quite wonderful. Mrs. Franklin laughed till tears ran down her cheeks, but at what Mrs. Betty could not tell for her life, and she grew more grave than ever; and then, beginning to think of poor Maitland, she became quite angry.

At last, Mr. Twisleden, at the silver voice of the time-piece striking ten, rose to take his leave; but Alice would only consent to his then going on condition of his drinking her health in a glass of fine old wine, of which she said she would send a bottle to his room. She had the butler summoned for that purpose, and ordered half-a-dozen into Mr. Twisleden's room.

" What a dear old creature he is !" exclaimed Mrs. Franklin, when he was gone.

" You will turn his head, Miss Franklin !" said Mrs. Betty, putting her netting by in its case, and speaking impatiently.

" Nay, dear Mrs. Betty, don't be out of humour," said Alice; " and I want to say something to you—do sit down again, dear Mrs. Betty."

The old lady sat down again, and thought, too, that she also wanted to say something.

" I wished to ask," said Alice, " whether you would have any objection to change your two rooms, Mrs. Betty ?"

Mrs. Betty looked at her in amazement. " Yes,

Miss Franklin," she said, " I should ; I may just as well be candid as not ; I should have a very great objection."

" I am sorry for that," said Alice ; " but I wish to mention to you an alteration I am just about to make."

" Never mind it, my dear, now," said her mother, seeing the cloud on Mrs. Betty's brow.

" I may as well mention it now as at any other time," returned Alice ; and Mrs. Franklin, who hated of all things to have disputes with her daughter, determined to hold her peace, and let Alice have her own way.

" It is best, Mrs. Betty," said Alice, " that we should understand one another at first. I wish to have no strife ; but I am mistress here. I am about to complete my suite of rooms ; yours adjoin my dressing-room ; I like the aspect of them greatly— though there is not much view, and though they are low, still they will be more convenient for me than any other. I have made my arrangements, Mrs. Betty," continued she, seeing that lady did not reply ; " and you will oblige me by making choice of two others. The late Lady Thicknisse's rooms are much better than yours—much loftier, and better furnished. It is my desire," continued Alice, after having waited half a second for Mrs. Betty's reply, but in vain— " quite my desire to make all things agreeable to you, but you must expect some little changes."

Mrs. Betty, who, naturally, was as amiable as most human beings, might, nevertheless, after a certain degree of forbearance, be roused up to a most determined opposition, and then she was as obstinate as she had been mild before; it was so on the present occasion. She listened to Alice, first in sorrow and then in anger, and at last made her indignant reply.

"After all that I have seen," said she, "I shall not easily be surprised at any changes you may think it fit to make; but one thing I can tell you, Miss Franklin, that when I give up my rooms, I leave Starkey altogether. I had rather have those rooms than all the rest of the house. They were the favourite rooms of my mother; I sat in them as a child; when I left school they were given to me as my own—they were mine during my brother Sir Sampson's life-time; my poor sister-in-law never thought of taking them from me; they have been mine for upwards of forty years; and I must say that I think it a great want of respect, not to say something more, that you, a young person and a stranger here, to whom every room must be alike, should think even of proposing it—say nothing of talking in the high strain of being mistress here. It is not becoming in you, Miss Franklin, let me tell you, but still it is no more than one might expect; for when a young lady will make herself a country's talk about a reprobate like Sir Lynam, and flirt with an old creature like poor Mr. Twisleden, and turn off a worthy lover like young Mr. Maitland, an old woman like me has no right to expect good treatment."

"Mrs. Betty!" exclaimed Alice, in great indignation.

"My dear Mrs. Betty," remonstrated her mother.

"No, Miss Franklin," continued she, regarding neither one nor the other, "I don't expect anything very great from you; but this I have a right to expect,

some little common decency and respect.—You
yourself invited me to stay here.' ' It shall be your
home, Mrs. Betty,' you said, 'as long as you live, and
I hope you'll never have occasion to regret my
coming here.'"

Alice attempted to speak, but the old lady continued.

"That was very pretty and well said of you, Miss
Franklin ; but it was no more than was right, seeing
I had no home but this, and the house was so much
larger than you could want for years ; and I shall
now consider any attempt to turn me out of my
rooms as a hint for me to go,—so, unless you really
mean that, say no more about it."   And with these
words, without waiting for a syllable of reply, Mrs.
Betty left the room.

Mr. Twisleden drank the health of the fair lady
his mistress in some of the wine she had sent him,
and, fairly beside himself with her flatteries, although
he never was fool enough to dream of her love, he
vowed, half drunk as he was, to live and die for her.

Scarcely was he up the next morning, when he was
surprised by a visit from Mr. Metcalf of Durham,
and received from him the astounding intelligence
that Mrs. Betty Thicknisse, and not the fair Alice
Franklin, was the present rightful heir of Starkey.
Mr. Twisleden said very little—his principal question
being as to the mode of Mr. Metcalf's making the
discovery ; on hearing which, he rubbed his chin and
seemed lost in thought.   Mr. Metcalf thought that
his brother lawyer knew something of this codicil
before, but as Twisleden did not tell him so, he kept
his thoughts to himself.   Mr. Twisleden accompanied
him to Durham ; and all that day, and the next, and

till the end of the week, he remained in that city
having long and frequent consultations with him, at
which Sir Lynam was mostly present.

It was now two days since Alice and Mrs. Betty
had their misunderstanding ; and in this time the dear
old lady had **repented of her warmth of temper.**—
The very fact of her having erred in temper made her
placable **towards Alice,**—made her almost, if not
altogether, **overlook her unkindness, and forgive the
unreasonableness of her desires.**

Alice knew, **or ought to have known,** how strong
local attachments are in natures like Mrs. Betty's ;
and it was cruel to distress or take advantage of an
inoffensive person like her, who had but few pleasures,
and who was the most unselfish of human beings.

Poor Mrs. Betty ! She was sorry for the hard
things she had said, though she still thought Alice
deserved all that had reference to her behaviour to
her lovers, including **the old lawyer among them; but**
so **sorry, nevertheless,** was she, that she was almost
inclined to give up her rooms, to show that she was
neither selfish nor unreasonable. **Alice, in the mean
time, was suffering from wounded vanity; and vanity
wounded, if it heal at all, heals but slowly.** She was
more determined than ever to show herself mistress
there, and she began **to turn over schemes in her own**
mind for getting rid of **the old lady altogether.**

Such were her thoughts, only in part unfolded to
her mother. One morning, **when Sir Lynam Thick-**
nisse was announced, she thought instantly of Mrs.
Betty's words, how she had made herself a country's
talk for a reprobate like him, and, as Mrs. Betty was
not present, she received him with something of the

hauteur with which she had taken leave of him. Sir Lynam chuckled in his own mind over her coldness, and thought how he should spread a snare about her from which she would not escape, unless she were far more disinterested than he took her to be. He assumed, therefore, a coldness equal to her own; apologised for his intrusion, which he said was only in consequence of his wish to prevent her receiving what he had to communicate through less friendly channels.

Alice grew almost pale, and Mrs. Franklin, starting to her daughter's side, exclaimed, "For Heaven's sake, Sir Lynam,—what have you to say?"

Alice thought of Maitland—perhaps they two had fought a duel and he was shot; and Mrs. Franklin thought of a suit for breach of promise of marriage.

Sir Lynam, in the mean time, coolly took half a sheet of letter-paper from his waistcoat pocket and laid it before Alice. It was a copy of the codicil of Sir Timothy's will, under which, in very few words, was written the legal opinion of Mr. Metcalf,—namely, that during the life-time of Mrs. Betty Thicknisse, Alice's right of possession was not worth an hour's purchase.

Alice neither screamed, nor fainted, nor fell into hysterics.

"What proof have I," asked she, in a tone of cool displeasure, "that this paper is worth anything?"

Her mother hastily glanced at the paper which her daughter held.

"We never heard before of any codicil to Sir Timothy's will,—and who is this Mr. Metcalf who thus obtrudes his opinion?" asked Alice, as Sir Lynam gave no answer to her first query.

"I will send instantly for Mr. Twisleden," said Mrs. Franklin."

"Mr. Twisleden is in Durham, my dear Mrs. Franklin,' said Sir Lynam speaking at once in his most friendly voice. "He is gone over in consequence of this astounding discovery."'

Whether it was that Sir Lynam's altered voice and manner subdued Alice, or whether it was the natural effect of her overwrought feelings, we know not—but, proud as she was, she sat down and burst into tears. This emotion, however, continued only a moment; but it is astonishing how different her manner was to Sir Lynam when she next addressed him. "It has been very kind of you," said she, "to prevent my hearing of this, as I might have done, from strangers; tell me now all that you know about it, and what is your honest opinion.—Did the late Lady Thicknisse know nothing of it, nor Mr. Twisleden?"

Sir Lynam leaned upon the table by which he was seated, and looked like Alice's best friend. "It is impossible for me to say," returned he. "what knowledge the late Lady Thicknisse had of this fact. My opinion, however, is, that she knew it, and that she destroyed the codicil to the will in her possession. As to Mr. Twisleden—" Here Sir Lynam paused and shrugged his shoulders.

"Good Heavens!" exclaimed Alice. "Do you think Mr. Twisleden is not to be trusted?"

"Mr. Twisleden," returned Sir Lynam, "was the confidential friend and professional adviser of Lady

Thicknisse, and he never betrayed his trust; he is no less worthy of your confidence—nay, indeed, he would serve you with a zeal he never could be expected to feel for your predecessor."

"And what does Mr. Twisleden say to this discovery?" asked Alice, taking no notice of the expressive half-smile which accompanied Sir Lynam's words, and which was meant to imply that Alice had unbounded influence over the old lawyer.

"He holds," returned Sir Lynam, "precisely the same opinion as Mr. Metcalf; there cannot be difference of opinion."

"But," asked Mrs. Franklin, "if the late Lady Thicknisse destroyed this codicil to Sir Timothy's will, how comes it that this Mr. Metcalf is become so learned on the matter?"

"To be sure!" said Alice.

"The probate-copy of the will," answered Sir Lynam, "retains the copy; Mr. Metcalf, either for curiosity, or in the prosecution of some law inquiry, examined this will in the ecclesiastical court in Durham, and made the discovery; he communicated it to me. He is a friend of mine, and wished to benefit me thereby; but the discovery avails nothing to me,—though it is of the most vital consequence to you. I sent over for Twisleden, and I assure you," said Sir Lynam, smiling again, "that the poor old gentleman showed far more distress and agitation than you have done.—'We'll secure it to Miss Franklin,' said he, 'spite of a dozen codicils—though,' said he, ' if this came into a court of law, not all the wigs and gowns in the kingdom could decide contrary to the will.' And Twisleden is right," added Sir Lynam.

And does Mrs. Betty know anything of this?" asked Alice, with an anxiety of manner which betrayed her feelings.

" Good Heavens! no!" returned he; "that would be absurd indeed."

Alice was glad Sir Lynam said so, for that was her opinion, though she was not quite prepared to say so.

" Mrs. Betty may live twenty years," said Sir Lynam, artfully; " it is Mr. Twisleden's opinion— her constitution is excellent, though she is not the wisest person living."

" Yes, certainly," said Alice, thinking to herself that if Mrs. Betty got possession of Starkey, and lived twenty years, she herself should be four-and-forty before she could again enjoy it.

" Certainly," repeated Sir Lynam, and added laughingly, that there was not the least reason in the world to tell Mrs. Betty about it. " The late Lady Thicknisse," he said, " had been quite right; Mrs Betty was not fit to have the management of a place like Starkey."

A servant at that moment entered, and said that Mrs. and General Byerly had called. " Not at home," said Mrs. Franklin.

The servant said, with the utmost politeness, that the ladies were not at home. The Byerlys saw Sir Lynam's groom leading about his master's horse, and they knew that he was there. They adopted, therefore, the idea that was universally prevalent, that the heiress was really receiving the addresses of Sir Lynam Thicknesse, which no little displeased them, for they themselves had a son for whom, in the

family arrangements, Alice Franklin had been fixed
on as wife.

Mr. Twisleden came next day from Durham.

He himself, as Sir Lynam had said, held the same
opinion as Mr. Metcalf, and he told Alice so with
tears in his eyes.

" Must I then give up Starkey ?" asked she, with
a deep sigh, which penetrated to the depths of the
old gentleman's soul.

" Not if our law-craft can keep it for you ; and I
think it can," replied he.

" I am mortified," said Alice, confidentially, to
her old friend—for twelve hours had passed since the
conference with Sir Lynam, and twelve hours often
set things in a very different light.—" I am deeply
mortified," said she, " that Sir Lynam knows so
much of this affair."

Mr. Twisleden shook his head, and said, " That
Mr. Metcalf was a friend and old associate of Sir
Lynam's, and that, after all, he thought it was a deal
better that the affair was known to him than to another less interested ; the most natural thing was to
make known this discovery to Mrs. Betty—this Mr.
Metcalf would not do—Sir Lynam had prevented
that."

So then Mr. Twisleden thought, as everybody else,
that Mrs. Betty must be kept out of possession.
That was Alice's secret opinion, but she did not avow
it, and she was glad that Mr. Twisleden prevented
the necessity of her so doing.

" I am sure," said she, " I know not what is best
to be done—I shall leave all to you. Do whatever

you think right—and with that I shall be quite satisfied, even if it be to resigning in favour of Mrs. Betty."

"We must keep terms with Sir Lynam," said Mr. Twisleden, "or we cannot be sure of Metcalf."

"Would not Mrs. Betty sell her right in Starkey?" suggested Mrs. Franklin, startled by her daughter speaking even of resigning in her favour, and not perceiving the ground on which this show of magnanimity was built.

"We will leave it all to Mr. Twisleden," said Alice, satisfied that Mr. Twisleden understood her.

Plans for circumventing Mrs. Betty and her rightful claims filled the heads, not only of Mr. Twisleden, but of Alice and her mother, though not one of all the three spoke out plainly to the other.

Alice slept not that night. It was the first sleepless night that she had passed at Starkey; for though she had laid long awake after parting with Henry Maitland, that affair gave her not half the distress of mind, not half the disturbance of spirit, which this did. To sink again into the poor Alice Franklin, with only a reversionary right to Starkey; to have to wait and wait for possession, year after year, till she was quite old perhaps—she could not bear the thought of it.

No! Mrs. Betty knew nothing of her rights; besides, what could she do with a place and an income like that of Starkey? It was absurd—it was ridiculous to think of it! No, no, Starkey must still be hers—and if the lawyers were not clever enough to suggest some plan of securing possession to her, she must suggest one herself!

M

It was a night of sore trial and temptation. Alas !
Alice was not strong enough to resist.

" No," said she, the next morning, surveying her
beautiful figure in the glass ; " mistress of Starkey I
am—and mistress of Starkey I will remain !"

Sir Lynam and Mr. Twisleden came that morning
together. There seemed to be the best understanding
in the world between them.

Mr. Twisleden said that Mr. Metcalf's silence
was secured—Miss Franklin need have no anxiety
on that score ; neither need she have anxiety on any
other—added he, with an expressive glance.

" I have suggested to Mr. Twisleden," began Sir
Lynam—

" Better that she knows nothing of it at present—"
interrupted Mr. Twisleden in an under voice. " You
will put yourself in our hands ?" asked he, addressing Alice in the most kindly manner; " we have your
full permission to act as we think well."

Sir Lynam's eye was fixed on Alice, and she was
mortified that spite of herself she quailed before it ;
she was again displeased that he knew so much of
her affairs ; she felt instantly that her consent to this
plan, whatever it might be, would put her in his
power ; and her pride was wounded.

" Give me till this time to-morrow, to deliberate,"
said Alice.

" My dear girl," interposed her mother, " I 'm
sure Mr. Twisleden will do nothing wrong ; you can
portion off Mrs. Betty very handsomely ; a day is
often of consequence in such things."

" We will only take care that Starkey is secured
to you," said Sir Lynam.

" *We*," repeated Alice, with offended dignity, and yet not loud enough for Sir Lynam to hear; and then addressing Mr. Twisleden, she said, " I will leave all my affairs in your hands, my dear sir—I am sure you will not compromise my honour;" and with these words, giving her hand to her mother, they two went out.

CHAPTER IX.

A WRONG THING DONE; AND AN EFFORT TO SAVE ONE WHO WILL NOT BE SAVED.

A DAY or two after this, Alice went into Mrs. Betty's room. She had made up her mind to dispossess the old gentlewoman of her rights; Mr. Twisleden knew that—so did Metcalf and Sir Lynam Thicknisse; and whilst she seemed always shy of the subject with any of them, she had been given to understand that all, without her interference, would be managed for her.

Into the exact state of Alice's mind we must not too narrowly inquire. She had taken counsel with herself, and had discovered that she could much better bear the reproaches of conscience regarding wrong done to Mrs. Betty, than she could support the humiliation and, as she thought, the disgrace of giving up possession. She said to herself, that if Mrs. Betty knew nothing of this her claim, the withholding her rights could matter nothing to her; and that after all, the late Lady Thicknisse was most

to blame, for she knowingly had deprived the old
lady of her legal right—while she herself had merely,
as an involuntary agent, taken what was given her.—
She said to herself, furthermore, that she had passed
the Rubicon in committing herself with Sir Lynam,
and that done, she was not now likely to turn back.

To Mrs. Betty, therefore, she went a day or two
after the misunderstanding between them, intending
to charm her by a great show of amiability and sweetness, even supposing that she persevered in her displeasure.

Poor, dear Mrs. Betty, to persevere in displeasure
was out of her power; she had, as we have said, forgiven Alice because of her own temporary wrath;
and had not Alice come to her with smiles of conciliation, she would have gone to her, and most
likely have offered up her two beloved rooms as a
peace-offering.

Never till then had Alice so much laid herself out
to please, and never till then had seemed to care at all
for Mrs. Betty; and the poor old gentlewoman's
heart warmed to her far more than if she had no
cause of displeasure against her.   Alice talked of her
uncle Netley and of Elizabeth Durant; of the life
she had led at Richmond, and of the life she meant
to lead here when Elizabeth, early in the spring,
came to visit her.

Mrs. Betty in the midst of all this was half inclined
to say a kind word for poor Henry Maitland; but a
message from Mr. Twisleden, requesting five minutes
conversation with Mrs. Betty on business prevented
it.

"Do not go, my dear Miss Franklin," said the

old lady, as Alice hastily rose to leave the room,
" Mr. Twisleden has no business with me that need
be secret from you. It is only about the legacy, I
know ; he sent about it yesterday ; so sit down, my
dear !"

Mr. Twisleden, Sir Lynam Thicknisse, and a
stranger entered.

" My friend, Mr. Metcalf," said Mr. Twisleden,
presenting him.

Alice was astounded as well as Mrs. Betty, for the
visit looked formidable. Alice's colour changed, for
she guessed the object of this, and with a feeling
akin to faintness she sank into a large chair in the
duskiest corner of the room, that she might be out of
sight of Sir Lynam.

Mr. Twisleden said, in the most business-like
manner, presenting a roll of bills before Mrs. Betty,
that there she would find six thousand pounds, the
produce of certain sales which had been effected according to the will of her late sister-in-law, which it
was the desire of Miss Franklin to have literally
fulfilled.

Mrs. Betty smiled kindly on Alice, Sir Lynam
smiled too ; but Alice saw neither one nor the other,
for she sat with her hands over her eyes, and felt for
the first time that she had consented to a villanous
action.

The gentlemen assisted the old lady, who never
had any head for business, to count up the money ;
and then, afraid of giving trouble, though she was by
no means at all sure of the fact, she said, "Oh yes,
it is right ! I am sure it is right, Mr. Twisleden. I

have the greatest possible dependence on you—I would take your word like gospel in any case!"

A lawyer has two consciences; the one his professional one; the other belonging to himself as man. This last conscience, in Mr. Twisleden's case, gave him an uncomfortable twinge just then; but then his professional conscience said, "All the better for us, my dear madam, that you have this dependence on me." Mr. Twisleden made no audible reply, however, to Mrs. Betty, but merely bowed and took a pinch of snuff.

Sir Lynam stood with his chin between his thumb and finger, and his eye fixed on Alice.

"I must just trouble you for one moment longer," said Mr. Twisleden, as politely as possible; "as one of the executors of the late Lady Thicknisse, we must trouble you for your signature of a receipt."

"A receipt in full," said Mr. Metcalf, stepping forward, and beginning to open a formidable-looking deed.

"Perhaps, Metcalf, you will just run it over, that Mrs. Betty may hear it," said Mr. Twisleden.

"Oh, there does not need that," said the confiding old lady. "I am sure it is all right, Mr. Twisleden."

"As a mere matter of form," said Mr. Metcalf; "it will not occupy many seconds;" and so saying, in the most rapid manner possible, he began to read over the contents of half a skin of parchment.

Alice knew the nature of it, and she felt sick as it went on to state, in the fullest manner possible, Mrs. Betty's renunciation of all right and title to Starkey, under the will of Sir Timothy Thicknisse

" Gentlemen," said Mrs. Betty, interrupting Mr. Metcalf in the midst of his reading, " I don't understand a word of what is being read—not one single word of it !"

" Nothing but a mere form—a mere form, I do assure you," said Mr. Metcalf.

" Well, I don't know," said Mrs. Betty, sorely puzzled ; " it's all right, Mr. Twisleden, I suppose."

" Quite right, quite right, my dear madam," said Mr. Twisleden ; and Mrs. Betty being thus pacified, Metcalf read on more thickly and more rapidly than ever, and Mrs. Betty, when he had ended, knew not one word of the latter part of the deed.

" This," said Mr. Twisleden, looking unusually pale, " is merely to secure the estate from after demands or claims."

" A mere form," said the brother lawyer, smiling ; " the law makes security doubly sure."

" Well, I'm sure I know no more about what I've heard than the child unborn," said Mrs. Betty, taking the pen which Mr. Twisleden presented to her between her fingers. " Did you understand it, Miss Franklin ?" asked she, turning to Alice.

" It is, you hear, merely a form," said Alice, thus appealed to ; and Mr. Twisleden, anxious to spare her, gently took hold of Mrs. Betty's hand which held the pen. " Perhaps you will be so good as to put your signature here," said he ; " Mr. Metcalf—Sir Lynam, you will be good enough to witness Mrs. Betty's signature."

Poor Mrs. Betty, as she said, knew nothing of the nature of that which she was about to sign, although

she could not help remarking, " I should have
thought a plain, simple receipt on a ten-shilling
stamp, or whatever the sum would require, would
have been quite enough—but," added she, "lawyers
know what they are about—so much money for so
many words—you'll find that out, Miss Franklin,
before long;" and with these words, which the dear
old lady meant for a little joke, she signed her name
before witnesses, and therewith, as the deed specified,
of her own free will resigned all right and title whatever to the property of Starkey.

"Let me congratulate you on secure possession,
my dear Miss Franklin," said Mr. Twisleden, meeting Alice an hour afterwards.

Alice did not choose to tell Mr. Twisleden what
her own conscience had said to her on the subject
within the last hour; and leaving him therefore with
the full impression that she was highly satisfied, she
went to dress for a quiet party of their acquaintance,
the Byerlys and the rest, who were going to dine
with her mother and herself that evening.

Scarcely anybody that was with them that evening
was as well pleased with Alice as formerly. Every
one thought her engaged to Sir Lynam Thicknisse,
and nobody liked him. She too was silent and abstracted, and never had appeared to so little advantage before. The fact was, she thought very little
about her guests; and though she had by no means
lost her desire to dazzle and captivate, she had not
any power over herself that night. "It is weak,"
thought she to herself a hundred times that evening,
" to think so much of this affair—for if I were to be

tried a thousand times I should still do as I have done, and with all these people here wondering at me—it never will do!"

She rallied herself for two minutes, and then for the next ten relapsed into dark thoughts: she had consented to a villanous deed—she had put herself into the power of Sir Lynam Thicknisse! A bad conscience is a most troublesome bosom guest; it will be heard, though a hundred voices be raised against it.

The next day Mr. Netley arrived at Starkey. There was a great show of welcome, and it somewhat reconciled Alice to herself to make the good old gentleman feel what joy his arrival could give.

Well, Starkey was a fine place, and Alice was very lovely, though looking, as he thought, somewhat paler than she had done at Richmond; and she seemed to become her station admirably, and had, moreover, received him with such overflowing affection, that, spite of all her fickleness to poor Maitland, he, her old loving uncle, could not help feeling proud of her, and satisfied with her too.

His old servant Jonathan told him wonderful tales of the ample kitchens and offices, butler's rooms and housekeeper's rooms, and of the number of old, respectable servants, who, having all just received their legacies, were in high good humour, and had all something to say in praise of their young mistress. Old Mr. Netley was no more than mortal, and so dazzled was he by his niece's grandeur, and so won by her show of kindness, that it was ten days, at the very least, before he was able to take a more sober view of things. By degrees, however, after the first dazzling view was taken, he began to see now one

little thing and then another which displeased him
Of Sir Lynam's visits he had heard before he came,
and of what the world said thereon—that indeed it
was which sent him at that season to Starkey at all;
but for the first several days the baronet had not presented himself; now, on the contrary, he came almost
every day, and there was a sort of understanding
between the two which greatly annoyed him.

Suspicion once roused does not readily sleep again,
and Mr. Netley now let nothing escape him: there
was a peculiarity about Alice in her intercourse with
Sir Lynam which he could not fathom; she was both
cold and confidential—there was an anxiety in her
manner when she was with him, and an uneasiness
and an impatience if she saw him in company with
others: she very rarely spoke of him, yet he had seen
her turn pale before him.   In Sir Lynam's eye, too,
there was an occasional glance as of triumph; he ex-
ercised a sort of arbitrary power over her; he would
fling a look at her in her proudest and haughtiest
moments, before which she would quail.   Mrs.
Franklin, too, showed him the most extraordinary
consideration: with her it was, "Sir Lynam, this;
and my dear Sir Lynam, that,"—just as if they were
the oldest and best friends in the world, or as if she
had her own particular reasons for paying him attentions.   The more the old gentleman looked on, the
more he was dissatisfied; he remembered all the
causes of complaint he ever had had against his niece,
more especially regarding poor Henry Maitland; and
he resolved to watch her more narrowly. He did so;
and what between his own observations, and his suspicions, he began to find that Alice was by no means

what she had been; her light-heartedness was gone; her very independence of action was gone. It was no use talking to her mother; there was something so specious about her too, he could not make the same impression upon her that he used to do.

It might be only the natural influence of all this wealth; but someway or other he thought there was a something more than that, could he but penetrate it. The only person who seemed to have any transparency of character about her was Mrs. Betty. He very soon made, therefore, a great acquaintance with her—or rather a great friendship, and referred to her to have all his perplexities cleared up.

But we may as well give Mrs. Betty's letter to Elizabeth Durant, written about a fortnight after this time.

"*Starkey, January* 24.

"My dear Elizabeth—I am just got up from a sick-bed, where I have been confined for five days, but more from sickness of mind than of body. Strange things have come to light, and others equally strange have taken place here, which have no little unsettled me, and of which what the end may be, God only knows.

"Mr. Netley, who seems to be a very straightforward, determined sort of character, took, it appears, an early opportunity of inquiring from Sir Lynam Thicknisse what were his intentions towards Miss Franklin. Sir Lynam, who has always failed in respect to the old gentleman, replied somewhat offensively, though without demur, that it was marriage, referring him at the same time to his niece. My surprise was not less than his when he informed me

that Alice herself verified this.   Sir Lynam had been
accepted by her for nearly three weeks.

" I have not words to express my astonishment—
not to say my distress—so beautiful as she is, so rich, and
so accomplished, she might have chosen from the very
best in the land ; and then to have hurried things in
such a disgraceful manner, scarcely three months after
her predecessor's death, to have given this preference to
the very man who insulted, as it were, her death-bed ;
scarcely three weeks, too, after breaking with poor
Mr. Maitland, and while she hardly knew whether
he was living or dead, to promise herself to such
a reprobate !   Heavens, Elizabeth, it is more than I
can understand !

" There had been some little disunion between
Miss Franklin and myself, but that was all passed ;
a better understanding seemed to be growing up between us ; she was one that I could not help loving,
spite of her faults, and I flattered myself that I might
even win some affection from her in return.   I had
made my will, after having received my legacy, and
had left her a little remembrance in it ; for though
anything I could leave would have been nothing to
her, still I wished to show her a mark of my regard.
I know not exactly how it was, but my heart seemed
warming to her, and she on her side, had behaved of
late with much softness and kindness to me.

" I could not help shedding tears when Mr. Netley told me the avowal she had made to him. ' Poor
thing !' said I, ' she knows not this man's character ;
she knows not her own worth, and how she might, if
she would only wait awhile, pick and choose from
the very best families in the county !'

" Mr. Netley, as I said this, rung the bell and ordered her to be sent to him, in my room, where we were sitting. She came, which was more than I expected, and, full of unspeakable indignation, he began to upbraid and scold her. That was not by any means the right tone to use with her; a proud crimson rose to her brow, and with the utmost coolness she told him that she was her own mistress, and meant, in her own time, to marry Sir Lynam.

" ' I will present myself before you at the altar,' exclaimed Mr. Netley, almost beside himself with passion, ' and forbid such an unholy wedlock !'

" Alice's figure seemed almost Titanic, as she rose up and with a look of concentrated anger declared, that ' neither Heaven nor earth should prevent it.'

" ' Oh Alice, dear Alice !' I cried, with tears in my eyes, ' you know not into what misery you are blindly rushing ! You know not the character of this man !'

" My words seemed to have an immediate effect on her passion. ' It is my fate !' said she, in a milder voice, and reseated herself.

" ' Alice,' said I, taking her hand, ' you are young, you are inexperienced; let me warn you—let me save you ! You know not your own worth, neither do you know the character of this man. You will espouse certain misery in marrying him !'

" The colour had died from her cheek as I spoke, and she burst into tears.

" ' You are a stranger in these parts,' said I, ' you know not Sir Lynam ; you gave your promise to him thoughtlessly ; withdraw it without a moment's delay !'

N

" ' I cannot ! I cannot !' said she, covering her face with her hands.

" ' You broke your promise of years to one of the best men on God's earth,' exclaimed Mr. Netley with great warmth, ' and one who loved you better than life, and yet you cannot break it to this profligate—to this lover of a day ?'

" ' I cann. t !' repeated she again.

" ' And why, in Heaven's name ?' inquired he, catching violently hold of her arm.

" ' It is enough for me that I know I cannot !' said she, disengaging herself, and speaking in a tone of determination.

" ' God in Heaven !' exclaimed he, growing more inflamed by her coolness.

" ' Alice, dearest Alice,' said I, ' give me a relation's privilege over you, let me persuade you to listen to reason and experience.'

" ' No, Mrs. Betty, no !' said she, putting me aside and rising, yet with tears in her eyes, which she endeavoured to conceal. ' My mother is satisfied, so am I too ; what needs it then that others should interfere ? If I do wrong it is myself alone that suffers ; I have taken a step which I cannot recall, and I will allow no one to interfere with my actions !' and with these words she left us.

" The old gentleman's anger was indescribable, and I was more hurt than I can tell. I really am become extremely attached to her, and her blindness fills my soul with compassion.

" ' It is infatuation ! it is madness !' said Mr. Netley, stamping on the floor with rage. ' This in· heritance has turned her head !'

" *Jan.* 27. So far, my dear Elizabeth, I wrote three days ago. I now take up my pen to continue my chronicle of events.

" The scene with Miss Franklin, as recorded above, and the distress and anxiety of her worthy uncle, quite overset me, and I have had again one of my fits of nervous head-ache, which has left me very much of an invalid. I needed, however, to have had more than my usual strength for that which awaited me— but not to keep you in impatience, I will proceed to tell you all.

" I had just taken my coffee in bed, yesterday morning, when the card of a Mr. Bartholomew, Solicitor, London, was brought to me ; he was quite a stranger to me, and refused to leave any message, begging most strenuously to see me. I dressed hastily and went to him, no little alarmed, as I always am, when lawyers come on sudden business.

" Mr. Bartholomew, who is a very large, imposing-looking person, entered upon his business without any circumlocution. The information he had to give me, would, he said, he doubted not, no little surprise me—as you may believe it did, when he informed me, that I—even poor I—the insignificant Mrs. Betty Thicknisse, was the rightful possessor of Star-key during the term of my own natural life ; in proof of which he produced a copy of a codicil to Sir Timothy's will. A great deal he said about the wrong which had been done to me by my late poor sister-in-law, who it seems, knowingly, or unknow-ingly, God only knows, kept me out of my own rights. I forgive her, and if she wrongfully possessed herself of what was mine, may God as freely forgive

her as I do.   I, it is possible, might not have had as
easy a conscience as I now have, if all this power and
possession had been mine.   There is deep meaning in
those words of our Lord's prayer, ' Deliver us from
temptation.'

" My head, at no time very clear, was in no condition to understand the wordiness of this Mr. Bartholomew, so I sent to request the favour of Mr.
Netley's company that he might give me some little
advice, for I take him to be a sensible, practical
person.

" Mr. Bartholomew was known to him by character.   The merest accident in the world, he said,
had thrown the will of Sir Timothy Thicknisse into
his hands.   He was down at Durham on some law
business, and had occasion to search some papers in
the Ecclesiastical Court, and giving the man a less
fee than he expected, was remonstrated with thus:
' Gentlemen,' said he, ' do not commonly give merely
a half-crown ; it was only yesterday that I received
a seven-shilling piece for a sight of old Thicknisse's
will.'   ' Ah so !' said the lawyer, recalling that case
of singular inheritance, and feeling a sudden desire
to see the will also, ' I too will give you seven shillings for a sight of that will.'

" ' I saw it,' said he, ' and was instantly struck
with the unacknowledged nature of the codicil ;
' Who was the gentleman,' asked he, ' who last saw
this will ?'   The man could not tell, excepting that
he believed him to be one of the descendants of the
testator—the present Sir Lynam Thicknisse.'

" ' Thank you, Sir ! thank you, my dear Sir !
exclaimed Mr. Netley all at once, as if he were out

of his senses; 'give me your hand; you have suggested an idea to me—you have done me the greatest
service!'

Neither I nor Mr. Bartholomew could, for the
life of us, tell what the old gentleman meant.

" ' My dear Sir?' said I.

" ' Yes, yes,' said he, ' We will go to law on this
codicil. Mr. Bartholomew, you shall undertake the
case.'

" Mr. Bartholomew looked all alive. ' There is
the best ground in the world,' said he, ' on which to
found the claim. Mrs. Betty Thicknisse has the
most indisputable title.'

" ' I cannot—I will not, disinherit her!' said I.

" ' You both can and shall!' exclaimed Mr. Netley. ' She shall be again without a penny, but in
reversion. You may live twenty years, Mrs. Betty,
and she shall marry poor Henry after all.'

" I began to see what his intentions were; in dis-
possessing her of Starkey, the affair with Sir Lynam
would be at an end.

" ' There is no doubt whatever about it,' said I,
as we talked it over again when Mr. Bartholomew
was gone. ' Sir Lynam's object is Starkey, and if
my putting forth my claim will save her from this
marriage I will do it. But understand Mr. Netley,'
said I, ' for myself I covet not Starkey. Two rooms,
peace of mind and rest of body, love to my fellow-
creatures and duty performed before God, are all I
covet, all I aspire to!'

" Oh, my dear young friend! you know not what
an agitation these things have thrown me into. My
heart warms to Alice, as it has never done before; I

feel as if I were about to injure her; but the Almighty is my witness, that were Starkey my own this very moment, and I could but know her free from Sir Lynam, I would resign it into her hands. She is far fitter for the mistress of this noble place than an old woman like me.

"But whatever I am, my dear Elizabeth,

"I am, and shall ever continue,

"Your true friend and well-wisher,

"BETTY THICKNISSE."

CHAPTER X.

PERSEVERANCE AGAINST HOPE.

MRS. BETTY and Mr. Netley had a long consultation together, in which they arranged their plan of action. On condition of Alice giving up the acquaintance with Sir Lynam Thicknisse, and binding herself not to marriage with him, Mrs. Betty should voluntarily resign all her claim to Starkey; but if Alice remained perverse, that the old lady's claims, the validity of which admitted of no doubt, should be strenuously asserted; Alice deprived of possession; and thus, though by unpleasant means, a marriage should be prevented which both the good old people were convinced ensured only misery and degradation.

Mrs. Betty, who felt herself inadequate to opening, by word of mouth, this business to Alice, of which she supposed her to be in ignorance, although there was every reason to suppose Sir Lynam was acquainted with it, wrote her a note, full of kindness and consideration, the penning of which cost the dear old lady many tears, and with which she inclosed a copy of the important codicil, begging to be allowed an interview with her at her earliest convenience.

Nothing, as may be expected, could exceed the dismay and consternation of Alice on reading this note, and her suspicions instantly fell on Mr. Twisleden; she believed herself to have been betrayed by him. Inevitable disgrace seemed before her; and she almost cursed herself in the bitterness of the moment.

"Better, ten thousand times, to have thrown myself on the generosity of Mrs. Betty! Oh, Heavens! that I had done so at once!" said she.

It was, however, the fear of detection and disgrace which wrung these bitter words from her; and, full of unspeakable resentment, she summoned her lawyer to her presence.

Twisleden received all her reproaches with the indignation of an innocent man, as indeed he was, regarding any betrayal of her; and Alice was too deep-seeing into human nature not to discover that Twisleden was too much her slave to have played her false. She gave him her hand; assured him again of her confidence; besought his forgiveness of her suspicions; and received from him, not only assurances of undying fidelity, but assurances, also, that after the deed which Mrs. Betty had signed, she, herself, was unquestionably secure of Starkey beyond the power of a thousand lawyers, and even that if the old lady were determined to contest it with

her, which he did not believe she ever would, the
greatest possible care should be taken that Alice, herself, was in no way compromised. Mrs. Betty was a
weak-headed person ; all the world knew that ; she had
signed a deed one day, of which she had repented
the next ;—or the nature of which, in fact, she
appeared quite to have forgotten. Nothing in the
world was easier than to deal with an opponent
of Mrs. Betty's character.—What he now counselled
Alice to do, was to treat the affair cavalierly,—to
set light by the codicil, and defy her, if she liked, to
do her worst. "There was nothing," Mr. Twisleden
said, "like carrying things with a high hand."

Greatly assured by the interview with Mr.
Twisleden, Alice gave permission for the interview
with Mrs. Betty.

Both ladies looked pale and agitated when they
met. Alice, prouder and colder than ever, as if she
had been injured ; and Mrs. Betty trembling with
emotion, and with eyes full of tears, as if she were
weeping over the pain she had to inflict.

"Dear Miss Franklin," began the old lady, after
taking the seat which had been indicated to her, and
seeing that Alice waited for her to begin ; "it is
impossible for me to tell you the pain which this
discovery has occasioned me!"

"It need give you but very little, Mrs. Betty,"
said Mrs. Franklin, who knew all, and was seated
by her daughter ; "resign your claims, if you really
have any, in favour of Alice, at once."

"That I will do," returned Mrs. Betty, who
found it much easier to proceed with the business
when she saw the tone they were about to assume ;

"that I will do to day, nay this very hour, on one simple condition."

" What is that ?" asked Alice, feeling instantly a determination to exert her utmost power of fascination, " you will ask no condition, dear Mrs. Betty, which I will not willingly grant ;—half my income —anything, dear Mrs. Betty, but the disgrace— or rather, I should say, mortification of giving up all. I am sure you understand my feelings;" said Alice, in her most winning tone, and looking with infinite affection on the old lady ; " to be a laughing-stock—a country's talk—oh, Mrs. Betty, I'm sure you will save me from that ?"

" I will save you from that, dearest Miss Franklin," said Mrs. Betty, earnestly ; " and I will save you from much more than that, from humiliation and misery ; from marriage with Sir Lynam Thicknisse !"

Alice started,—clasped her hands and was silent.

" Gracious Heavens !" exclaimed Mrs. Betty, " what fascination is this! Sir Lynam the spend-thrift, the libertine, the hypocrite ! Alice," said she, " you have not known him for years, as I have done ! In marrying him, you unite yourself to misery ! Mrs. Franklin," said she, addressing that lady ; " can you, her mother, calmly see this, and not interpose to save her ? Ten thousand times better would it be, to descend to poverty's self, even had she been ten times richer than the possession of Starkey made her, than marry this man ! You are young, Alice ;" continued she, " you are beautiful, you are made to win all hearts, and if your mother will not act a mother's part by you, to save you from worse than mere poverty—I will;

and not a mother's part only, but the part of a
stern teacher—I will take Starkey from you—and
thank God that I have the power of doing so—and
then see if Sir Lynam will marry you!"

Under other circumstances Alice's good sense
might have whispered that there was truth in Mrs.
Betty's words, but she was then in no humour
to make acknowledgment or concession even to
herself; she remembered Mr. Twisleden's words,
and felt angry that a person like Mrs. Betty should
use this tone of assumption—as she chose to deem it;
she remembered that he had counselled her to carry
things with a high hand, and she determined to
follow his advice.

" I myself will break with Sir Lynam Thicknisse,
if I see fit," said she, " without the compulsion or
interference of any one; and as to Starkey, if you
have a right to it, Mrs. Betty, assert it; you will
find me quite ready to defend my claim. Mr. Twisleden himself advises me to give up merely what the
law demands."

" I am an old woman," returned Mrs. Betty,
meekly; "and to go to law, and to get into notoriety
of any kind, would be most unpleasant to me, would,
I should consider, under ordinary circumstances, be
very unseemly and disgraceful: but, Miss Franklin,
this I will do:—the first lawyers in the kingdom shall
take my cause in hand; I will get possession from
you, and not one sixpence shall reach you till the
Almighty takes me hence, and in his sight it will be
a righteous deed!"

Both Alice and her mother seemed speechless.

" Yes, Alice," continued Mrs. Betty, speaking in a

voice of strong emotion, "this I will do, and from the warmest affection for you! Heaven knows what it is from which I would defend you; from tears and heart-ache on earth, and it may be from endless misery hereafter; for what may not a tyrannical wicked nature like him tempt you to? Oh, Alice," said the poor old gentlewoman, dropping on her knee before her; "give me your word before witnesses not to marry this man, and I will sign the fullest deed of renunciation; and, fondly though my heart clings to this place as my home, I will go away to-morrow, and never trouble you more!"

"Rise, rise, Mrs. Betty, rise!" said Alice, really moved, spite of pride and every other bad counsellor, by the disinterested spirit of the old lady; " I cannot bear this : I am sure you mean well to me. Give me till to-morrow to consider!"

Mrs. Betty rose, and kissing Alice's forehead, left the room unable to say another word.

Sir Lynam that day had a long consultation with the two lawyers, Twisleden and Metcalf. He was the accepted lover of Alice; he was privy to the trick which had been put on Mrs. Betty, and, looking on Starkey as his own already, he considered himself entitled to take part in every movement.

Sir Lynam all this time seemed the most gentle-manly of men; and but that Mr. Twisleden knew what the baronet's character was, and what his conduct had hitherto been, he might have considered him a very pleasant, although certainly not a very high-principled man.

All was satisfactorily arranged among them. The utmost confidence was felt on their part regarding

Alice's claim. The first lawyers in London were to be consulted and employed if the cause came to trial: their opinion, however, was that, considering the odium of an old person like Mrs. Betty advancing her claim in opposition to one with so many recommendations as Alice, who in a few years, sooner or later, must come into possession, she would before long come to terms with them; sign another deed of renunciation; and thus, aft·r the lawyers had all made a nice thing of it for themselves, there would be an end of the matter, without their being in any way committed. All the odium would fall on Mrs. Betty, and the young heiress would, as it were, only have additional claim to universal favour.

Poor Mrs. Betty! after her interview with Alice, she had a terrible fit of nervous headache, and it required all Mr. Netley's determination, and strong-minded clearness of purpose, to keep her in harmony with herself.

· "I'll get the affair fast into the hands of the lawyers," said he to himself, " so that she can't run off; for, spite of all her prejudice against Sir Lynam, I am not quite sure whether Alice may not over-persuade her; and, as I'm a living man, after she has broken with Maitland, she shall not marry that fellow if human power can prevent it !"

Mr. Netley, therefore, engaged Mr. Bartholomew. who was a lawyer of great talent and reputation, and determined that, if on the morrow Alice's determination was to abide by her engagement with Sir Lynam, that he would return immediately to London, and, as agent for Mrs. Betty, lose not a moment in prosecuting the suit.

Sir Lynam Thicknisse was at Starkey that evening, but he left again without seeing Alice; she refused to see him on the plea of indisposition, and somewhat chagrined he rode away again, after exchanging a few commonplace compliments with her mother. Not a word was said or hinted to him of Mrs. Betty's proposal.

Alice sat alone that evening in communion with herself; she passed a sleepless night; and when the next morning dawned upon her, her mind was as little settled as it had been the evening before.

" I wish," sighed she to herself, " I could see my way clearly and definitely before me !"

What were, in fact, Alice's true sentiments it is not very easy to say. Love for Sir Lynam ? No, certainly—not at least such love as that which young Maitland had cherished for her—it was a vague sort of undefined, uneasy passion, half self-love, which had in the outset desired his admiration, and coveted influence over him, and which, now that it had been gratified, she could easily have given up for any new object; but then the step which self-interest had made her take regarding Mrs. Betty, and which had been suggested, and urged on, and brought about by Sir Lynam, had placed her in his power—had made her fear to break with him. A secret injurious to her honour was in his keeping. Suppose she were to embrace Mrs. Betty's proposal—what then ? She had already secured her own firm hold on Starkey : Mrs. Betty might threaten, but Alice was assured by her lawyers that she had put all power out of her own hands; and if she were to break with Sir Lynam, it would be only unsealing his lips to trumpet abroad

o

her own disgrace, for she could well believe Sir Lynam
capable of taking deep revenge. Poor Alice! she
flattered herself, as many a woman does, to the rivet
ing of her own misery, that she should retain as much
influence over the husband as she had had over the
lover, and she determined to risk all.

"There are men I might love better than Sir
Lynam," thought she to herself, "but I cannot
retract; I am too deeply committed with him for
that. I may risk something in marrying him, but
I am eternally disgraced if I make him my enemy!"

That day, therefore, her answer went to Mrs
Betty. She could not allow herself to be dictated to,
she said, "although she gave Mrs. Betty credit for
the best intentions towards her, and that on deliberate
consideration she found no occasion to interrupt the
connexion existing between herself and Sir Lynam
Thicknisse."

It may naturally be asked—as it was, and that in
no very measured terms by Mr. Netley—Whatever
Alice's mother was about, to let her run blindly on
her ruin?

"Bless you, my dear sir," said she, in reply, "what
can I do? Alice is old enough to judge for herself:
she has always shown great good sense; and if I were
to turn her this way or that way, how can I be sure
that it would be for the best? It has always been
my opinion that parents have no right to dictate and
control in cases of this kind. Our children marry for
themselves, and not for us; and I have this confidence
in Alice, that she will do nothing without sufficient
reasons, though she may not choose always to communicate them."

The fact was, Mrs. Franklin sacrificed her own judgment to her daughter; to use a common phrase, her head was turned with her prosperity; she could hardly believe that the mistress of Starkey could do wrong. She had been weakly silent in the trick upon Mrs. Betty; and having been silent then, she felt as if she had not any right to speak afterwards.

Alice's decision made an irreparable breach between herself and her uncle; and impatient to make her feel how in earnest was the threat of dispossession, he hurried to London, with full authority from the almost heart-broken Mrs. Betty to set lawyers at work against her.

"Let nothing of all this alarm you," my dear Miss Franklin," said Mr. Twisleden, as the first letter from Mrs. Betty's lawyer was laid before her. "You are as safely in possession as if the old lady had been dead a dozen years."

"We must have the park-wall continued round that part which is called the Pleasaunce," said Sir Lynam, as he drove Alice and her mother out one fine morning early in April, for he began even to speak of everything as if it were his own. "I will return that way and look at it; there is good brick-clay down there, and we will burn our own bricks."

Alice made no reply; indeed, she had not heard his words. She had been thinking, of what now and then would come across her thoughts in those pleasant spring days, that Elizabeth Durant must think her unkind never to write to her, especially as she had talked so much of her visiting Starkey early in the year. "But how could I have her with me?"

thought she again, as she always did on such occa-
sions. "It is quite enough that Mrs. Betty and I
are at variance."

"Oh, my dear!" said her mother to her, "have
you mentioned to Sir Lynam about our going into
Scotland?"

"Not before grouse-shooting?" said Sir Lynam.

"As soon as ever the weather is settled," said
Alice. "I would have gone to London, but someway just at present I cannot bear London; and till
this affair is settled with Mrs. Betty, it is unpleasant
to be in the same house with her."

"I think she ought to have withdrawn," said Mrs.
Franklin; "two people in one house who are at law
with each other. It is quite ridiculous!"

"I mean to take a house in Edinburgh," said
Alice. "I have a great desire to see the beautiful
scenery of Scotland. Oh, it will be so quiet there!"
said she, with a deep sigh, forgetting—poor Alice!—
that where the mind is not at ease, there is quiet
nowhere.

Sir Lynam turned and looked at her, and for the
first time was struck with the anxious expression of
her countenance.

"Yes, very good," said he, thinking of the Highland scheme, "and I'll come up for grouse-shooting."

CHAPTER XI.

A BROKEN HEART.

LAWYERS are not remarkably speedy in their movements, for a reason very sufficient to themselves; that a long job pays much better than a short one.

Mr. Bartholomew and Philip Durant, who was the counsel chosen for Mrs. Betty, met many and many a time to talk it over, and to deliberate as to what was next to be done; seeing that Alice's lawyers, from whom they confidently looked for offers of compromise and conciliation, stood aloof and seemed as if they made sure of having the most firm ground of right. All this time Alice's lawyers had, on their part, made themselves quite sure that, however determined Mrs. Betty, urged on by Mr. Netley, might be, that she never would suffer the thing to come to a decision by law. Month after month, however, went on; the spring came, and the summer and the lawyers of Mrs. Betty made not only no step to pacification, but gave notice for the cause to come on in autumn.

Alice and her mother, meantime, were in Scotland, whiling away the pleasant summer months among the most beautiful Highland scenes; Alice finding wherever she went admirers and friends, and creating an interest for herself, not only as the so-much-talked-of heiress of Starkey, but also for her own personal attractions.

"Oh! how heavenly would this life be," sighed she, "if I could only forget Starkey!"

But we must turn back from summer months and Highland scenes, to the early part of February, when Nehemiah Netley, having arrived in London full of grief and displeasure against his niece, went to inquire after Henry Maitland.

"And how is Henry?" asked he, from Maitland the elder, who, with a sunny tradesman's smile on a sad countenance, was bowing two titled ladies out of his shop.

"He'll never be himself again," returned he, his countenance growing sadder and more troubled; "never, as long as he lives, Mr. Netley. I'll tell you what," continued he, growing at once very red, and looking very positive, "if it had not been for the promise I made him when I thought he lay on his death-bed, if it had been my last shilling I would have spent it in having revenge; in making her one way or other repent of it!"

"My dear sir," said Mr. Netley, "she's laying up repentance for herself, as fast as you or her worst enemy can wish it!"

"And no more than right, Mr. Netley" returned the other; "as a man sows so shall he reap; and I've no reason, not I, to wish any good to her. It makes me downright angry, to see what a wreck she's made of my poor boy!" and spite of his anger, Mr. Maitland wept; but ashamed of the emotion which he could not control, walked into a little private room behind his shop and fairly sobbed aloud; Mr. Netley the while stood midway in the shop, looking tolerably unmoved, but experiencing, nevertheless, feelings not much less bitter than those of his friend.

"I'll tell you what, Maitland," said he, going into the little private room, when he thought the father's emotion might be somewhat abated, "I'll tell you what I've been thinking of; there's nothing like change for a mind diseased. It will never do to let him mope at home over his troubles; we must do something to amuse him."

The two old gentlemen sat down and talked it over. Mr. Netley, always active, and always liking above all things to be employed for somebody or other, proposed to take charge of him during a tour somewhere.

The Peace of Amiens had just then been concluded, and all the world was flocking to Paris, which then, when the Continent was so little known to the English, offered of course more novelty even than now. To Paris, therefore, the old gentleman offered to conduct his young friend, and to Paris they went.

The letters which he and his companion wrote were cheerful and interesting, and the happiest results were anticipated. They staid for a month in Paris, and then Henry, who seemed to have a repugnance to returning to England, proposed that they should venture still farther, even though the Continent was anything but in a settled state. Maitland, however, spoke French admirably; and by steering their way through those states of Germany which were in alliance with France, they penetrated much farther than the English generally did in those days.

They were soon in Saxony; and Mr. Netley, who

had always had a great interest and curiosity about the Moravian settlements, proposed that they should visit the great mother-colony of that people at Herrnhut. All was alike to Henry Maitland; and, somewhat wearied and over-excited by travel, and the anxieties of travel in those times of trouble and ferment, he too began greatly to long for quiet. Chance had thrown them in the way of a certain Graf Sternberg, who was nearly connected with the family of the Zinzendorfs; and furnished by him with letters to the principal elders of the community at Herrnhut, they travelled direct thither.

Like a peaceful island in the midst of stormy waters lay the little settlement of these " Watchers of the Lord," as they called themselves, in the midst of war-shaken Germany. It was a summer's evening when they approached the place; cultivated fields covered the hill-sides, and good roads cut through trim plantations—the work of the early settlers, under the direction of Count Zinzendorf,—gave the most cheerful character to its locality. Presently they overtook a band of peasants returning from their field-labour, who were singing a hymn of thanksgiving. The very air seemed to the travellers apostolic; and as they drove quietly into the village itself, the clean, cheerful exterior of the houses, the breadth of the well-paved streets, the pleasant gardens which they saw here and there, and the broad walks, which seemed leading into pleasant wildernesses, all together made such a striking contrast to the aspect of all other German villages, as diffused a gladness over their spirits. The farther they advanced the more they were favourably impressed, and

pleased : no noisy children were quarrelling in the
streets ; no disgusting figures of poverty and wretch-
edness met their eye—they saw only healthy-looking
men with cheerful yet serene countenances, and mild-
looking women in the quiet garb of the sect, all
wearing caps of the most snowy linen, tied with
ribbons of various colours, denoting the wearer to be
maiden, wife, or widow. Music, too—not the gay
waltz or warlike melody, nor even those stirring na-
tional airs almost universal to Germany, but music of
a soft devotional character—was heard from many an
open window which they passed, or from gardens
where men and women, and little children, had
assembled for worship or social enjoyment.

"Thank God !" said Henry Maitland, laying his
thin, feverish hand on the arm of his friend ; " we
have at last found the right place—at last found a
haven of peace ! Oh !" said he, as if his soul were
at that moment unlocked, " you know not how I
long for rest—rest, even if it be that of the grave !"

" Yes, yes," said Mr. Netley kindly, who was
accustomed to his companion's low spirits, "this is,
indeed, a blessed place, and we will stay here as long
as you please ; but you must not give way to low
spirits, for this is not a gloomy place, you see."

The excitement of travelling had greatly fatigued
Henry, and the quiet of Herrnhut was like a balm
to his spirit. They took lodgings in the village, and,
presenting their letters of introduction, were received
not only by the distinguished persons to whom they
were addressed, but by the whole community, as
brethren. It was a remarkably fine summer, and
week after week rolled on, if not to the strengthening

of Henry's mind, at least to the apparent soothing of it. One or two things, however, occurred to excite Mr Netley's anxiety: in the first place, whilst his companion's general amiability and sweetness of manner, which were in him natural characteristics, seemed to have increased, there was a certain wilfulness at times about him which defied the old gentleman's management. Again, whether it was from the influence of the religious atmosphere, as one may say, of the place, or the mystical books which since he had been among the Herrnhuters he had read, or whether it was the natural effect of his own unhappy mind preying on itself, we know not, but there seemed to hang over him a dark cloud—half fanaticism and half melancholy—which affected his whole demeanour. He professed to be happy; he fell into no religious disputations, but lived among the pious people who surrounded him in the interchange of good offices: but still his mind lay under a dark cloud which no kindness could penetrate. These things made Mr. Netley anxious; but then, on the other hand, his physical health was much improved; and the excursions which he made on foot, especially into that mountainous district on the north of the Elbe called the Saxon Switzerland, and which was at that time rarely indeed trod by the foot of an Englishman, proved his bodily strength to be much greater than it had been.

Nothing, therefore, gave Mr. Netley more satisfaction than that his young friend should make excursions of this kind, particularly in company with the intelligent and excellent young men of the community. Henry Maitland also had gone to Dresden; gone there to his sorrow—but why so, **poor youth!** he never told to his friend.

Dresden in those days was not what is now; but even then it was in possession of its noble picture-gallery, and which **from the first day of** Henry's entering it, became his place of favourite resort. Groups of gay fluttering people were not, **as now,** seen circulating through **it.** A casual traveller visited it now **and then, or a** solitary painter sat undisturbedly **day by day** copying his favourite picture. Here **too** came Henry Maitland daily; but it was not a Rubens that brought him here, nor a Correggio, nor was it the divine **beauty of the** Sistine Madonna: the picture that **riveted his soul,** and before which he stood with folded arms and abstracted melancholy gaze hour after **hour, was the** St. Cecilia of Carlo Dolci.

Unhappy youth! There was, or he fancied there was, some likeness between the subject of this picture and Alice Franklin; and thus that passion, which time and absence might perhaps altogether have conquered, woke again in all its intensity, and many a time, after standing **for hours** before this picture, he would rush from the **gallery** with feelings akin to madness.

All this, of **course, he told to no one** — least of all to Mr. Netley; and when the old gentleman **would** propose to accompany him next to Dresden, this was always zealously opposed, and, jealous of his **friend's** even suspecting his state of mind, spite **of his haggard,** melancholy countenance, he assumed a cheerfulness of manner which, if it did not impose upon his friend, at least pacified him.

It **was now the** beginning of August, and Mr.

Netley, who, however, carefully avoided ever speaking of Mrs. Betty's lawsuit before his companion, was beginning to think of his return to England on its account.

They were sitting together one evening, as they frequently did, in the lofty Watch-house occasionally used for worship, and which overlooks the quiet burial-ground of the Herrnhuters. It was a lovely scene; the harvesters in the near fields were singing as they cut and bound up the corn—and an old white-headed Hernhuter, seated on the tomb of old Count Zinzendorf, was expounding the Scriptures to a group of little children that had gathered round him. It was, indeed, a lovely scene; the warm evening light shone over all, like an emblem of the beauty of holiness; and whilst Nehemiah Netley looked down from the Watch-tower over all, tears filled his eyes. "Willingly, most willingly would I," said he to his young friend, "end my days here—lie down and sleep with the good people who slumber there, and rise with them again at the resurrection!"

Maitland sat with his head upon his hand—he made no immediate reply, but a sigh, nay, almost a groan, escaped him. "There is a new cemetery in Dresden," said he after a few seconds, "which pleases me more even than this—and if I die soon, let me be buried there—promise me," said he, almost solemnly. "There is quietness there equal to this, ampler space, and shrubs and flowers."

"Oh, you shall not die out of England, my good fellow," said the old gentleman, interrupting him, and speaking most cheerfully; "neither you nor I will die out of England!"

They came down from the Watch-house, and left the burial-ground, and as they walked homeward, Mr. Netley began to speak of their return to England, which he wished to take place in about a week. It was a subject Henry entered on reluctantly, and now he was bent upon another excursion to his favourite scenes of the Saxon Switzerland; he would set off, he said, the next day. His friend made no opposition. Henry had hitherto returned from such an excursion with increased vigour both of mind and body; and it was quickly arranged that he should set out next day with his knapsack for his farewell pedestrian ramble, and in the mean time Mr. Netley should make all needful preparations for their final departure.

"Take care of yourself, my dear fellow," said he at parting, "and may God bless you!" added he, kissing his cheek; not that he either admired or had adopted that primitive German mode of leave-taking, but he loved the young man as if he had been his own son.

Poor old gentleman, he never forgot that parting to the day of his death!

What Maitland's feelings were during this unhappy excursion, none but the Almighty knows: many things afterwards were remembered of him and talked of. His road lay among scattered villages, and as travelling in those days, and especially in those parts, was by no means common, everywhere the handsome young foreigner with the melancholy countenance had been seen; and what was remarkable is, that every anecdote that was related of him denoted amiability of character, and kindness of heart—which afterwards helped no little to console his old friend.

P

He sat and talked with a young soldier, who was suffering from his wounds, by his mother's door, and even helped, in the absence of the surgeon, to replace bandages which had fallen loose, and thus contributed to the sufferer's ease; he gave money to a peasant family who sat weeping amid the ruins of their house, which had been burned down; and in the beautiful valley which lies between Schandau and the Kuhstal, he was seen directing the steps of a blind man who had no one to guide him.

Thus, for several days, he was seen by one and another—was seen too in the various points of attraction in this lovely region. There were not then, as now, guides at all these several places to point out this and that, and relate the old and interesting traditions of the district: all at that time was wild and solitary, saving for the native dwellers of the place. These became aware, in the course of a few days, that a melancholy stranger was among them, who either sat with his arms folded, and his eyes fixed on the glorious scenes around him, yet with an abstraction of demeanour that showed his mind to be far away, or else he was seen hurrying along from place to place, as if in eager quest of somewhat. Kindly peasant women told how they had offered him a draught of milk and a slice of bread, as at other times he had been seen slowly passing by, as if worn-out with fatigue; and told, too, how at their addressing him he had seemed like one suddenly woke from a dream, taken the refreshment they offered, smiled sadly, and then hurried onward.

Some thought him feeble from sickness; some thought him insane; but all agreed that he was unhappy: and the experience of sorrow is so universal, that though he opened his heart to no one, he found everywhere sympathy and kindness.

How his mind, however, worked all this time, or preyed upon itself, it is impossible to say. Solitary communion with nature, while it heals some wounded hearts, only aggravates the suffering of others;—it was so, we must suppose, in poor Henry Maitland's case.

One early morning, while all nature was calm and beautiful, dew on the grass, flowers on the earth, and joyous birds in the trees above, a peasant woman and her boy, passing through the woods at the foot of the great Winterberg, beheld the saddest spectacle which mortal eye can see—a lifeless human form— youthful, but dead,—lying among the grass and flowers.

"Dear Lord!" said the boy, "it is the good gentleman who, only yesterday, gave money to poor Fritz!"

The woman raised the head; but though she, too, had recognised the dress, she could not see the features for the tears which blinded her eyes.

We cannot, if we would, describe the agony of poor old Mr. Netley, when, instead of the return of Maitland which he expected, he was summoned, by the police regulations, to attend to the melancholy event which we have just recorded. Poor Maitland had died by his own hand, for the pistol which had effected his death was still clenched in his hand.

Good old Mr. Netley; of all the troubles which his life had ever experienced, this was unquestionably a thousandfold the saddest! He felt almost unable

to communicate it to Maitland's family ; the youth
had been entrusted to his care, and this was the end
of it.

But we cannot pretend to write of his distress; we
will only tell that neither his prayers nor his tears
could obtain that a German law should be relaxed in
his case. Henry was adjudged to have died by
his own hand, and could not be buried in holy
ground, for the good man had had the body removed to Dresden, and fondly had desired to fulfil
his unfortunate friend's melancholy wish to be buried
in the new cemetery there. To Herrnhut, therefore,
he returned—what a melancholy, heart-breaking
return !—and amid the tears of the good people,
who had loved the unhappy youth as a son and
a brother, he was laid among their dead, in their
" Gottes Acker," or field of God.

All affairs in England had now lost their interest
for him ; he cared neither for his niece nor for
dear Mrs. Betty and her lawsuit, and gladly would
he have ended his days among this quiet, unworldly
community, and slept at last beside his unhappy
friend,—but it could not be. Fearful rumours of
war came from far; terror and gloom sat on the
countenances of all men ; and late in the year,
after shedding plenteous tears over the grave of his
poor friend, he returned, without any announcement
to any of his friends, not even Maitland's family,
to his house in Richmond, where he shut himself
up as a recluse.

CHAPTER XII.

A KIND HEART WOUNDED; AND A WEDDING THAT LOOKS GAY.

THE summer wore on, and both parties of dis-
putants respecting Starkey said that the affair
would be settled by trial in the autumn. As the
autumn approached, however, Alice's lawyers began
to feel a little uneasiness, because Mrs. Betty's
lawyers remained so calm and confident; and Alice
herself, who had grown morbidly sensitive on the
subject, began to console herself with the hope
that even if, at last, her own lawyers were obliged
to confess the act of treachery to which she had
consented, both Mrs. Betty and her uncle, however
much aggrieved and displeased they might be, would
still spare her character, by never permitting it
to be made public.

Towards the end of the summer Mrs. Betty wrote
thus to Elizabeth Durant :—

" I live here as solitarily as if I were the dweller in
an enchanted castle; my neighbours however, the
Byerlys, and other good families of my acquaintance,
show me much attention, and would have shown
me more, had I not been too much out of spirits
to see company.

" This hateful lawsuit has, of course, occasioned
much talk; but it is a satisfaction to me that no one,
not even poor Miss Franklin's greatest admirers,
blame the part I have taken. She has lost her

popularity here, through her connexion with Sir
Lynam, which is the most singular instance of
infatuation that ever was known. Handsome he
unquestionably is, and he has conducted himself
decently of late; but then his character, his former
life, his want of principle, prevent people having
any reliance on him. I will be bound to say
that she never heard a noble sentiment proceed
from his lips—nobility of sentiment is not in him;
but he has an off-hand, dashing sort of manner,
that I suppose has taken her fancy. Poor Alice!
Nothing, as Mrs. Byerly says, will bring her to
her senses but the loss of Starkey; for then something of his true character will reveal itself. It
is Starkey that he wants, and not Alice! The
Byerlys, I take it, have been much disappointed,
on account of their eldest son not succeeding with
her. He was a fine young man, and is now just
about going to the West Indies for a couple of
years.—There would have been some chance of
happiness and respectability there.

" I hear from the Maberlys, who are just returned
from Scotland, that Sir Lynam is gone there for the
grouse-shooting. Alice and her mother have had, for
the summer, a fine place somewhere near Perth; they
lived there quietly, I am told, and somebody who
saw Alice said how pale she is looking. She is not
happy, poor thing! When this affair is settled, and
she has done with Sir Lynam, as she will the moment
I get my claim established, I shall give all up to
her, tying her, of course, off marrying Sir Lynam.
I have consulted with my lawyer on the subject, and
have already had a draft of the necessary deed drawn

up; for I don't want Starkey, or any advantage whatever, for myself. I should be ashamed of seeing myself in possession of this place, to her exclusion. She interests me greatly, and with all her faults, I have conceived an affection for her, and would, if possible, excite the same sentiment in her towards me. If we once get the spell of this unhappy connexion with Sir Lynam broken, all will be so different! Her natural good sense will soon show her how much her friend I have been. She will then soon connect herself worthily, for there is not a family in the county that would not be proud of an alliance with her. Poor thing! I hear that she speaks with severity of me; perhaps that is no more than natural. I can bear it for the present—in process of time she will know me better, and, I trust, love me too.

"I am impatient for Mr. Netley's return. He wrote me about ten days ago that he meant to be back for the trial. He is an excellent, strong-minded man, and without him I never should have had strength to have undertaken what is now in hand."

Towards the end of August she wrote again thus:—

"The time for terminating this terrible law-business approaches. Alice and her mother have left Scotland, and are now located on the banks of Windermere. The Byerlys, too, are in the lake-country for the autumn. Mrs. Byerly has been so good as to write to me: she is shocked, she says, with poor Alice's appearance, she is so thin and pale. You do not know how this has affected me.

"Sir Lynam has been here; he brought workmen to make alterations in the grounds. It was, he said,

by Miss Franklin's orders, but that I did not believe,
I was extremely incensed, and ordered both him and
his men off the place.   I did not think I could have
done so, having no one but the servants to stand by
me.   Twisleden is in London, and even had he been
here, I question how he would have acted—he seems
not to be the man he was in my poor sister-in-law's
days ; he is no friend of mine, that is the fact, and,
as is but natural, I have lost all dependence on him.
Well, I discharged Sir Lynam and his people, for-
bidding them again to set foot within the premises.
Sir Lynam merely smiled and bowed, and turning to
his workmen, said, ' A few weeks would make but
very little difference ; Miss Franklin would be here
herself in that time,' he said, ' and would give her
own orders.' So all went away. Mr. Twisleden, too,
had ordered a brick-field to be opened at the lower
part of the park ; that too is now stopped. They are
beginning, I imagine, to have some little apprehension about their rights.

    " You will be glad to hear that all the old servants
behave most kindly and faithfully to me.   All have
received their legacies, and most of them are thus
comfortably provided for life.   All, however, have
volunteered to remain with me when my rights
here are established.   If Sir Lynam comes here as
master, all will leave ; this, Mrs. Wardle, who has
taken upon herself the office of my woman—Lord !
to think of me having a woman, who, for nearly sixty
years, have done all for myself ; but so it is ; and it
is quite as well, for Miss Franklin thought her too
old-fashioned for her maid—she tells me that this
was respectfully intimated to Miss Franklin before she

left. Poor deluded creature! when even servants
have done thus, has she not had enough to excite
suspicion ?"

Whilst Mrs. Betty had the pen in hand which wrote
these words, a letter came by post from Elizabeth
Durant, containing an account of the melancholy
event recorded in our last chapter. The old lady
wrote no more that day, nor, indeed, for many days ;
her feelings were akin to those of poor Mr. Netley ;
she cared neither for herself nor her law-suit. What
were any troubles of hers in comparison to those of
her friend Netley — to those of poor Maitland's
family? And then the unfortunate youth himself
—what had he not borne, when grief at last had
brought on madness and suicide !

Hearts bleed and break, and all that while the
business of life goes on ; people eat, drink, sleep,
quarrel, become reconciled, or go to law to make the
quarrel worse, and never think all the while of what
others are enduring. So it was now ; while all this
master-sorrow was preparing which was to affect
more or less both contending parties, they were busied
about their own concerns, thinking them of interest
beyond any other.

The time which was to terminate the law-suit was
at hand, and Alice's lawyers began to be almost desperate under the continued silence of their antagonists,
who, as they learned, were in full preparations for the
most determined maintenance of their claim. A third
party then, prompted by Alice's agents, spoke of
compromise : but no! Mrs. Betty's lawyers would not
compromise one tittle excepting on the already proposed terms, which were rejected for Alice.

Sir Lynam Thicknisse was in London; in three days the trial came on; and Mrs. Betty's lawyers, well pleased with the evident anxiety of the adversaries, smiled in security.

"It never will come into court, however," said Philip Durant to Mr. Bartholomew, the very day before that fixed for the trial; "Miss Franklin will drop Sir Lynam rather than lose Starkey: we shall hear from them to-day."

Scarcely were these words out of his mouth when Metcalf and Twisleden were announced. Philip Durant and his fellow-lawyer exchanged looks of triumph. The two lawyers, however, came with no offers of compromise; but, as they said, by the desire of Sir Lynam Thicknisse, who had full permission from Miss Franklin to direct her affairs, they came to throw a new light on the whole affair; to lay before them " Mrs. Betty's deed of relinquishment to all and every of her claims on Starkey, under the codicil to the will of Sir Timothy Thicknisse."

"There is some collusion here! The thing is morally impossible!" exclaimed both Philip Durant and Mr. Bartholomew, in the same breath.

" Gentlemen," said Philip Durant, fixing a keen, penetrating glance on both lawyers; "this deed has been obtained by no fair means!"

"Make your best of it," said Metcalf, with a smile of successful craft; "we will leave a copy of it with you."

"Of course, gentlemen," said Mr. Twisleden, "you will not take this cause into court to-morrow?"

" Not to-morrow," said Philip Durant, " but early in the next term; for, gentlemen," said he, " I will plainly and fearlessly say, whoever may have been the agent in this affair he is "—a villain, Philip was going to say, but he merely added, " the law will not support him in it."

" This very hour," said Philip Durant to his disconcerted companion, when they were again alone, " I will set off to Starkey. This deed has never been obtained by fair means ; it will postpone the suit, but it will not be lost through it. It bears date but a few days before we received our instructions ; they never will suffer this deed to come into court."

Mr. Bartholomew saw a long perspective of fees before him in this prolonged cause, and it is hard to say whether he was not better pleased that new difficulties had sprung up to prevent the speedy termination of so rich a cause.

Philip Durant knew nothing of the suicide of poor Maitland : the news had only just then reached England in the newspapers, which as yet had, out of respect to private feeling, withheld the name; the letter, however, from Elizabeth Durant, bearing the tidings to Mrs. Betty, had reached her but a few hours before the sudden arrival of her London barrister was announced.

" Ah, Mr. Philip," said she, " I am in no state to enter on business, let it be as urgent as it may. The lawsuit is ended either for or against me—that is what you have to say—but after this sad news which I have just told you, it is strange how indifferent I am about the whole thing."

Philip, however, as a lawyer, looked upon the object of his mission as of really more importance to Mrs. Betty than even the awful death of poor Maitland, which nevertheless had affected him greatly, and at length he induced her to listen to what he had to communicate.

Philip laid the copy of the deed, bearing date the 10th of January last, before her, and explained its nature. " Had you knowledge of such a deed as this ?" asked he.

" I knew not at that time," said she, " that I had such right and title to Starkey ! About that time it was that I gave a receipt, a receipt in full, as I was told, for six thousand pounds of legacy under the will of my late sister-in-law."

" The same," returned Philip Durant: " it is included in this deed."

" O my dear sir !" said poor Betty in a voice of extreme distress of mind, after she had communicated to him all the particulars of the signing of that deed ; " there's an end of it, let the thing drop. This is the saddest part of the whole affair ; let her marry him, for she has deceived me cruelly, and one who could be party to a deceit like this is a fit wife for Sir Lynam Thicknisse. I have lost my interest now in trying to get Starkey. From me she received nothing but kindness ; I loved her and wished her well, but she has deceived me !" and overcome by these painful thoughts, the dear old lady wept bitterly.

" What with one thing and another," said she, after a while thinking of Maitland's death as well as Alice's deceit, " I cannot, my dear sir, do any thing more to-day. Leave me now, and to-morrow I will see you again. I shall be calmer then."

It was in vain that on the morrow Philip Durant represented to her, that considering the circumstances under which she had signed this deed, her true claim to Starkey was not invalidated. This deed might, in fact, he said, be taken rather as an evidence of fear on their part than anything else. It was in vain that he said this and a great deal more; her zeal for her own interests was cooled.

"I wanted not Starkey," said she, "for myself, but for Alice, and that by gaining it thus, I might be able to save her from ruin and misery, which I did not think she deserved; but the charm is broken. I have been deceived in her, she is less worthy than I believed; a struggle with a person of this character will cost me my peace of mind. Let her take Starkey, for which she has sold her honour—I will not contend it with her. I have, thank God, enough to provide for my wants while I live; I will leave Starkey to her, and let her find in it what peace she may."

To Philip Durant, as a lawyer, all this was a most undesirable mode of argument. The great law-suit was at an end; in the first step they had been out-witted, and now their client refused to proceed. It was very unsatisfactory; and he knew that Mr. Bartholomew would be even less pleased than himself, for he would neither sympathise, as he could, nor respect the poor old gentlewoman's mode of reasoning: more especially, disturbed as her mind was at the present moment by the death of young Maitland, and the mournful absence of Mr. Netley, who, in the outset, had been the mainspring of action.

"It is no manner of use, my dear sir," said she again to him, "your staying here and reasoning with me. I have made up my mind, and shall not stir another

Q

step in the business. Miss Franklin, as I tell you,
was herself party to this deed by her presence when
it was read to me. I could not understand it as a
mere receipt for my legacy; I appealed to her about
it, and she assured me that it was all right. Sir Lynam
Thicknisse was a witness to it in her presence; they
two were leagued together in it, and this is the
saddest part of the business. This explains his
influence over her—her blindness, as I thought it,
and her infatuation! You know not how all this
hurts me ; I had expected better things from her—
I thought her blind, but I never suspected her to be
wicked. Oh ! Mr. Philip," said she, unable to proceed, "it has quite overset me!" And Mrs. Betty wept
tears, such as a guardian angel might shed over a
wilful human sinner.

" No, Mr. Philip," continued she again, " my
mind is made up, and it is no use your wasting
your time here, and on me. A lawyer's time," said
she with a half smile, " must be paid for ; it is a
costly thing, and now I have done with Starkey, I
am not rich enough to afford the purchase of it."

Philip offered her his hand, and said that as a
lawyer he would not trouble her with his presence,
but as a friend was there nothing he could do for
her ? Philip had long been interested in her as the
fast friend of his cousin Elizabeth ; what he now had
seen of her interested him still more, and he sincerely
wished to be of service to her, and to show her
kindness.

Mrs. Betty considered for a moment, and then
replied, that as yet her immediate plans of action
were undecided. Her mind was not yet calm enough

to see what was best for her to do, but that, if she
needed a friend, she would not forget that she might
look for one in the friend of her beloved god-daughter.

Whilst this was going on at Starkey, there was
a show of rejoicing in an elegant cottage on the
banks of Windermere.

The people who looked on and saw what was
going forward, said, that a rich baronet was come
from London to marry the beautiful young lady
who lived there with her mother. The servants
of the family told what the baronet's valet had
said, that his master brought some great good—
news with him; that a lawsuit was ended all in
favour of the beautiful heiress, and that now she
would have thousands and thousands of her own,
which some envious old aunt or grandmother had
been keeping her out of, and that she would now
be married to her lover, from whom tyrannical
attempts had been made to separate her; that now
they would be married, and then go to her own
grand home, from which she had been for long
time an exile, living in humble cottages like some
heroine of romance.

It was a fine, interesting story, this, which was
told, and of which nobody entertained any doubt,
when, two days after the baronet's arrival from
London, they really were married, with every show
of happiness, village girls scattering flowers before
them, and village bells ringing, till the sunshiny
air, as it lay on the mountain sides and on the
lovely lake, seemed thrilling with happiness.

That, however, was but the outward show of
things.

On the morning of Alice's marriage, half-a-dozen gay people, friends whom the Franklins had made in their summer sojournings, breakfasted with them; among whom was the clergyman who was to perform the ceremony.

He and the father of Alice's two fair bridesmaids stood together in the window talking. They were talking of what did not, to them, seem a fit subject for a bridal morning—of an unhappy suicide, in the midst of scenery which, it was said, resembled that which surrounded them. Alice, as she sat in her bridal attire, caught a word—a name which riveted her attention—and then another word and then another—the two spoke in an under-voice and rapidly, for the wedding-procession was just about to set out. "I have the paper in my pocket," said the clergyman. "I will show it you when we return."

" Terrible! most terrible?" said the bridesmaid's father.

" What is terrible, papa?" asked one of the young girls, drawing on her white gloves.

" Nothing, my dear, nothing," said her father; " only a young fellow who has shot himself for love."

Alice felt as if she should faint. " For Heaven's sake," said she to her mother, " give me a glass of water."

No one but her mother saw her agitation, and she knew nothing of the cause of it. Alice thought of poor Maitland's broken ring, and of the last letter he ever wrote her; and whilst she thought of these things, she was handed into the carriage which conveyed her to church.

" How pale and ill Lady Thicknisse looks !" said
every one on the wedding day. Somebody, too, saw
her take up the paper which the clergyman had taken
from his pocket on his return from church, read
something, and then suddenly leave the room ; but
nobody knew, not even her mother, and least of all
her bridegroom, what a bitter agony was in her
heart.

Not many days after her marriage, Alice received
the following letter from Mrs. Betty Thicknisse :—

"However much," said the letter, "you may deserve
my reproaches, you will hear none from me. I have
endeavoured to save you from certain misery, but in
vain ; you yourself have prevented it. You have
deceived me : what I deplore most is, that I have
been deceived in your character. You have gained
Starkey, and if you can have peace of mind in having
thus gained it, I am still farther deceived.

" Oh, Alice, you have done cruelly wrong—but
most wrong to yourself! Endeavour now to amend
what is done ; and when your conscience wakes and
reproaches you for baseness and unkindness to me,
seek forgiveness from Heaven; and know, that though
I shall still weep bitter tears over you—still that I
have forgiven you. Why indeed should I not ? for,
God help you ! you will have brought such a punishment on yourself, as no malice of mine could have
wished you.

" You are now, I hear, a wife. A new life and
new duties are before you. Lead not your husband
into error : but oh! above all things, be not led into
error by him. Strive with yourself to ennoble and
purify your own heart, that if God give you chil-

dren, they may at least have one guide that they may follow.

"I leave Starkey to-morrow, my home for more than sixty years. Alas! this has been a hard struggle! I hope, when you are as old as me, you will know no pang like this, of leaving an old beloved home.

"In this world we shall probably meet no more. Our next meeting may be before the judgment-seat of God. Live so, Alice—dear Alice! I must say, for I love you!—live so that we may meet unabashed before His face.

"Yours in affliction, which however is but of time,
"BETTY THICKNISSE."

THE END.